He wasn't a white-picket-fence guy.

She was already overwhelmed with the personal relationships in her life. She didn't have the emotional bandwidth for more. And when she'd asked him for a break, he'd just walked instead.

They'd never exchanged promises. No words of love had come from either of them.

"Something *has* changed, though, Charlotte." He looked down at her stomach. "We're expecting a baby."

She clenched her fists to keep from covering her expanding belly protectively. And perhaps to keep herself from reaching for him, throwing herself against his rock-solid chest and breathing in the familiar scent of him. She needed to keep things between them civil and as distant as possible to protect her from temptation. "I'm well aware. I'm glad you want to be a part of our child's life, but we have five months to hammer out those details."

Declan extended one booted foot and lightly teased at the toe of her high-top. "It would be much simpler to discuss those details if we move in together."

Dear Reader,

Storytelling offers me the joy of creating characters with skills I dream of having but simply don't possess—like gardening. Yes, I can keep the grass alive, and I've found a few plants that are kill-proof. However, a "yard of the month" award is far out of my grasp. So needless to say I had a blast filling the pages of *The Lawman's Surprise* with thriving floral creations by the heroine, landscaper Charlotte Pace.

Thank you for picking up the latest novel in my Top Dog Dude Ranch series! I truly enjoy visiting with readers online, and links to my different social media accounts can be found on my website, catherinemann.com. Stop by to say howdy and perhaps share about your latest gardening exploits!

Happy reading,

Catherine Mann

The Lawman's Surprise

CATHERINE MANN

Recycling programs for this product may not exist in your area.

ISBN-13: 978-1-335-72452-6

The Lawman's Surprise

For questions and comments about the quality of this book, please contact us at CustomerService@Harlequin.com.

Harlequin Enterprises ULC
22 Adelaide St. West, 41st Floor
Toronto, Ontario M5H 4E3, Canada
www.Harlequin.com

Printed in U.S.A.

USA TODAY bestselling author **Catherine Mann** has won numerous awards for her novels, including both a prestigious RITA® Award and an RT Reviewers' Choice Best Book Award. After years of moving around the country bringing up four children, Catherine has settled in her home state of South Carolina, where she's active in animal rescue. For more information, visit her website, catherinemann.com.

Books by Catherine Mann

Harlequin Special Edition

Top Dog Dude Ranch

Last-Chance Marriage Rescue
The Cowboy's Christmas Retreat
Last Chance on Moonlight Ridge
The Little Matchmaker
The Cowgirl and the Country M.D.

Harlequin Desire

Alaskan Oil Barons

The Baby Claim
The Double Deal
The Love Child
The Twin Birthright

Texas Cattleman's Club: Houston

Hot Holiday Rancher

Visit the Author Profile page at Harlequin.com for more titles.

To my delightful daughter-in-law Shelley.
Thank you for teaching me how to
work decorating magic with magnolia leaves.
Love you!

Chapter One

Charlotte Pace wasn't a morning person.

And pregnancy had made her double down on those feelings.

If only she could just lie under the covers and nurse the saltine crackers for another half hour until it was time for work. But the insistent knocking on her cabin door couldn't be ignored.

She swung her feet to the floor and gripped the edge of the mattress, willing her crackers and flat ginger ale to stay down. Fingers curled into the plush mattress topper and the flower-patterned quilt. Her doctor assured her the nausea would likely ease in her second trimester, but right now she didn't feel on the upswing to better. A deep breath later, Charlotte stood, thankful she didn't have to search for a robe since she'd fallen asleep in an overlong T-shirt and a pair of running shorts—drawstring loosened to accommodate her three-month baby belly.

Another round of knocking echoed through the two-bedroom cabin.

Too bad her teenage brother who lived with her couldn't be bothered to roll out of bed up in his loft room. His surly attitude grew worse by the day since he'd started living with her. She'd known becoming his guardian four months ago when their mother entered a psychiatric facility would be difficult. Her brother—Rory—had always been a handful. But she'd had no idea how out of control he'd become. She wanted to sit down with him, talk things out... But at the moment, that went on the list of things she just didn't have the time or energy for.

Fishing under the iron bed, she found her favorite gardening Crocs, the once-bright daisy pattern dulled long ago. Still, she associated them so strongly with gardens that she smiled just at the sight of them. Her soul sang when she had her hands buried in the earth. She'd majored in horticulture in college. Now, she was head landscaper at the Top Dog Dude Ranch, the Smoky Mountain Tennessee soil giving her the perfect canvas to create.

She'd left her previous—better-paying—job for the position at the Top Dog Dude Ranch to help her mom. The job came with a flexible schedule, a cabin and access to the ranch's meal plan—a bonus since even last year her mom was already struggling. That flexibility sure would be stretched to the max after the baby arrived.

Worry dumped acid on her already churning stomach.

Crocs in hand, Charlotte stood while her fluffy pup uncurled all twelve pounds of herself from the floral quilt. Covered in long white-and-black fur, Primrose was some kind of Maltese mix with expressive brown eyes.

"Rosie girl, do you think you could run over to Rory's room and scratch on his door until he wakes up?" Charlotte stuffed her feet in her shoes. "We shouldn't be the only ones up so early."

The dog tipped her head to the side, showcasing a thatch of fur tied with a pink ribbon. Primrose jumped from the mattress, to the bench at the foot of the bed, then to the floor, tail wagging in a fan of fur as she waited by Charlotte's feet.

Kneeling, she straightened Primrose's bow. "I know, girl, I love you, too." Standing, she left her bedroom and wove around the sofa, calling out, "Hold on. I'm coming."

And Primrose kept on trotting alongside her. Not surprising. She was the epitome of a Velcro dog. Thank goodness she could come to work with Charlotte or the pup would grow so anxious she would chew holes in couch cushions and pull the stuffing out.

Tiny dog nails clicked along the planked floor. Charlotte hadn't been able to resist painting the nails pink.

Like a little girl.

A lump lodged in her throat as she wondered about her own baby. Taking in a dog two months ago probably hadn't been the wisest move, given she'd just found out about the pregnancy. But when she'd gone to visit her mom, she'd discovered that her mother had a new roommate at the psychiatric center who had been despondent over losing her pet. Worse yet, her kids had dropped off the senior dog at the shelter.

Even knowing her life was already too busy, Charlotte had made a detour on her way home. Just to look at the pup. Simply to reassure the women that her dog was fine. Hoping the pet had already been scooped up by some wonderful family. Only to learn that at nine years old, little Primrose didn't stand much of a chance of finding a new forever home.

The second she'd seen Primrose sitting all soggy in her water bowl, Charlotte had been hooked. Even the name *Primrose* seemed like kismet for a horticulturist like her. Sure, she didn't need a dog. She was overwhelmed with her job, the pregnancy, caring for her brother and her mom.

But she wanted Primrose. Her heart was still broken from her failed relationship with her baby's father. Seeing Primrose made her smile for the first time since Sheriff Declan Winslow had walked out of her life a month prior, their breakup irreparable. She'd hoped having him called up for National Guard duty would give her heart the time and distance to heal.

She'd been wrong.

"Primrose, stay," she told the dog, unlocking the dead bolt and swinging the door wide.

Only to have her breath catch in her throat.

Her brother hadn't answered the door because he hadn't been in his bedroom. Rory was standing on the porch, shuffling his feet behind Moonlight Ridge's very own Sheriff Declan Winslow. Her baby daddy. Back in town, not that he'd bothered to tell her. Looking too tall, lean and handsome in his tan uniform, with his wide-brimmed hat held against his broad chest. His hair was trimmed even shorter, no doubt from his Guard time.

Her mind echoed with strains of their final fight. While she knew he was an honorable man, she'd gotten frustrated with the way he always held back a part of himself. Then he'd told her he wasn't the white-picket-fence, family-man type.

Words that still squeezed her heart.

And with her waistline expanding, she was fast running out of time to tell him that family man or not, he was going to become a father.

Declan Winslow had struggled to find a way to let Charlotte know he'd returned from National Guard duty. In all the half-baked plans he'd made, he sure hadn't expected it to look like this. Standing on her porch bringing her delinquent brother home.

A phone call would have been better, yet he'd procrastinated. Now, here he stood, struggling to maintain objectivity in the face of her rumpled appeal. Her blond hair was tousled, a long T-shirt grazing her curves.

Deep blue eyes studying him with wary suspicion.

He deserved that. He wasn't proud of the way he'd broken off their relationship, but he didn't regret it. He wasn't the man for her. Not by a long shot.

A little furball of a dog shot through the door. A stray? People dumped their animals at the ranch far too often. The Maltese mix ran circles around Charlotte's ankles, leaping back and forth over her Crocs, drawing Charlotte's attention away. Snapping the thread of tension. Declan drew in his first full breath since he'd laid eyes on her.

The scent of mountain air, of a spring morning, filled his lungs. Small-town Moonlight Ridge, Tennessee, was his home and he loved it. Although being sheriff now that the Top Dog Dude Ranch was expanding brought a host of complications to his job with so many tourists. At least the ranch honored the landscape and the values of the area.

Charlotte knelt to scoop up the dog, cuddling it close to her chest before meeting his gaze again. "What's wrong?" She angled toward her brother. "Rory? Is everyone okay?"

Declan gestured to the ranch guests beginning to trickle from their cabins to greet the day. "Do you mind if we step inside? We're, uh, garnering quite a bit of attention out here."

"Of course," she said nervously. "Thanks for noticing. The last thing I want is gossip in my workplace."

Nodding, he gestured to her brother, who carried his teenage attitude like an imaginary overstuffed book bag slouching his posture and slowing his steps. "After you, kiddo."

Rory shot him a scowl before his gaze slid away and he shouldered past. "I'm not a kid."

The teen was no doubt using defiance to cover up the fact that he was nervous. And he should be. Declan wanted to clap him on the back and reassure him, but he also knew it was time for this teen to meet tough love. He'd gone too far this time, way beyond just sneaking out in the middle of the night.

Declan followed the boy over the threshold and inside. The cabin looked much like others at the ranch, with log walls and a rustic decor. But the space carried the imprint of Charlotte as well, in the arrangements of dried flowers filling the air with hints of lavender and evergreen.

His eyes drifted to the white sofa with her pink floral throw blanket, a phantom image of the two of them sharing stories late into the night drifting into his mind.

A defeated sigh brought him back to the present.

Charlotte cradled the dog closer, fidgeting with the bow on the canine's head. "So clearly Rory snuck out again."

Again? "It was more than just slipping out." He steeled himself for what he would have to say next, hating that it would hurt her. "Rory was caught breaking into the Top Dog gift shop."

Her knees folded and Charlotte dropped to the sofa, floral throw pillows spilling away. "Rory, what were you thinking?"

The teen shrugged, staring at his untied high tops, laces covered in mud and speckles of paint. His lanky body radiated surliness. But Declan knew from experience that was likely a blanket to cover a more vulnerable emotion.

Charlotte's hands shook as she stroked the dog repeatedly, as if for comfort. "Oh, Rory. You've pulled pranks before. But breaking and entering? Potentially theft? This takes things to a whole other level. One that can ruin your future."

"It's no big deal," her brother said belligerently. "Everybody does stuff like that. It's just kid stuff."

Charlotte's mouth dropped open and she blinked fast, her eyes stunned, before she set her jaw in a firm line. "I thought you weren't a kid."

Growling, Rory pivoted away and stomped up the steps to his loft bedroom, slamming the door.

"Rory," she called out, standing. "Come back down here."

But the door stayed closed. The music started. Loudly. Dried flowers vibrated ever so slightly.

Sighing, Charlotte swayed, then reached behind to brace herself as she sat again. Worry creased her already weary face.

Declan understood her worry—and he shared it.

Rory was a kid in crisis, teetering on the edge of no return. He needed an intervention.

Sooner rather than later.

Declan hooked his hat on an antler coat tree on the wall. "I would let him cool off for now. It'll give us a chance to talk."

"Um, thank you. For bringing him home." She stayed seated, holding the pup close like a comforting pillow against her stomach. "And I'm sorry you had to deal with him."

Declan sat in a fat leather chair across from her. Sitting beside her would be too risky. Too tempting to reach out and comfort her. He needed to embrace professional distance. "Rory didn't take anything." This time. "He and his friends—Truitt and Kai—were painting graffiti on a wall. The alarm went off in the shop, which alerted the police department. I was at the station, so I took the call. Rory and I both tried to call you, but it went straight to voice mail."

Declan hadn't dated Charlotte long, only a few months, but long enough to be a part of Rory's life. To get to know him, to see firsthand how he was struggling with the move, sneaking out at night and hanging with the wrong crowd. And Declan hated the feeling of failure right now, telling him that he should have seen this coming. Should have been able to prevent it. That he'd let the teen down by not staying in touch after the breakup.

She chewed her bottom lip. "I was worn out and had the ringer off. Lucky thing you were back in town," she said, with a tinge of accusation in her voice. "I realize this could have been worse."

Maybe he should have called to tell her that he was back, but it wasn't like they were a couple anymore. They hadn't spoken since he left town.

Until this morning, he hadn't thought about how that would have affected Rory too, feeling let down by another adult that waltzed out. "I know he's a good kid at heart, but I can't help him much longer if he doesn't find his way to a serious course correction soon."

"Understood." She pressed a hand to her forehead, her face turning even paler. "I'm not making excuses. I get that I need to do better."

"*Rory* needs to do better." He leaned forward, elbows on his knees. He hated that she was taking the burden of this all on herself. "You've done nothing wrong."

An awkward silence settled between them, here in this room where they'd spent evenings with her cuddled against him on the sofa, a fire in the fireplace, a bowl of popcorn—extra butter and a sprinkle of cayenne pepper—in her lap while they watched a movie.

She fidgeted with the dog's paw, her thumb stroking the pink polished nail. "I didn't know you'd gotten back."

"I returned about a week ago."

Surprise flickered across her face. And something else. Disappointment? Once again, he kicked himself for not figuring out a way to let her know he'd returned. Not that he expected to pick up where they'd left off. She'd asked for a break, a breather, and instead, he'd ended things completely.

He cleared his throat and pointed to the furry scrap. "New stray at the ranch?"

"No, I adopted her from the shelter. Her name's Primrose." Charlotte smoothed her fingers over the graying fur on the dog's muzzle. "She's nine. I was worried no one would take her."

Signature Charlotte move. A big heart for the strays in life, like him.

He was treading into dangerous territory here. Back to business. Declan sat straighter in his seat. "So, returning to the problem at hand with Rory."

"What happens now? Is there going to be a court date?" Her voice went higher, her fidgety hands landing on a pack of crackers on the end table, gripping, twitching. "Do I need to get a lawyer?"

"No lawyer needed. Rory got off lucky." He didn't know many people who would be as forgiving as the Top Dog owners had been. That small-town community spirit—looking out for a neighbor, giving people second chances—was a large part of what drew Declan to leave the big city and take the job here, even if it paid less. Some things in life went beyond any price tag. "Hollie and Jacob said they don't want to press charges. They asked me to reassure you they don't blame you and this will have no bearing on your job."

"Seriously?" Her blue eyes went wide, long lashes sweeping upward. "That simple?"

"Yes. And no." He waggled his hand. "Jacob wants Rory to do volunteer hours to show he's sorry."

"That's all? No time behind bars? No court-appointed community service?"

"More of an informal community service. Each kid has been assigned a different task—we figured less time together might be warranted. Truitt will be picking up trash and Kai will be painting over the damage in the shop. Rory will muck out stalls in the stables."

Her mouth twitched. "He would probably rather go to juvie."

A chill settled inside him. "Not if he ever toured the place. Trust me, this is a cake walk comparatively."

She reached out. "I didn't mean—"

"It's okay. I understand what you meant. You've been woken up fast to a difficult situation with no morning cup of coffee." He knew how she woke up slowly, needing two cups of java on her front porch to greet the day. There was still so much he remembered about her—and now that they were face-to-face, he realized he was doing a lousy job of making himself forget. Telling himself that he was getting over her had been a lot easier with distance between them.

"It was an…unexpected way to greet the day. I wouldn't have minded an extra half hour, that's for sure."

It struck him again how tired she looked, pale,

Allen County Public Library
Telephone Renewal:(260)421-1240
Wednesday November 29 2023 02:48PM
Website Renewal: www.acpl.info

Barcode: 31833080125005
Title: His unlikely homecoming
Due date: 12/20/2023 23:59:59

Barcode: 31833080164384
Title: The lawman's surprise
Due date: 12/20/2023 23:59:59

Barcode: 31833082834299
Title: Maverick's holiday homecoming
Due date: 12/20/2023 23:59:59

Barcode: 31833082649762
Title: The rancher's Christmas reunion
Due date: 12/20/2023 23:59:59

Barcode: 31833080157859
Title: Fortune's dream house
Due date: 12/20/2023 23:59:59

Total items checked out: 5

holding on to her dog for dear life. Concern tugged at him. He wanted to ask how her mother was doing. If Charlotte was taking time for herself.

But that wasn't his business anymore. He pushed to his feet. "I haven't told Rory about the arrangement. I figured he needed to sweat for a while. I'll be in touch later today to make sure everything's all set with the O'Briens."

"Thank you again. I don't even want to think of how bad this could have been if you hadn't been the one to catch the call and smooth things over." She stood, swaying for a moment, before continuing, "I don't know what I would have done if I lost my job."

Unable to resist, he cupped her shoulder. A simple touch. Plenty of space between them. Her eyes held his, her gaze filled with so much worry it was all he could do not to haul her to his chest and reassure her again that all was well with the owners of the ranch. They were good, fair people.

Like Charlotte.

She deserved better than he had to offer. Better than him.

Backing a step away from her before he said or did something they would both regret, he swept his hat off the coatrack. "Try to get some sleep. You're looking pretty..." Pretty. Just pretty. "Looking pretty exhausted."

Chapter Two

Could this morning get any worse?

Charlotte hip-bumped the door closed after Declan, all too aware that she looked like death warmed over, while he was as ruggedly handsome as ever. But that was the least of her worries.

Rosie licked Charlotte's chin as if reminding her she wasn't alone.

"I love you, too, Rosie." She dropped a kiss on the pup's head. "What are we going to do about Rory? Huh?"

Was shoveling out stables going to be enough to set him back on the right path? If so, she would make sure that barn was cleaner than ever. And thank goodness each of the kids responsible would be given a different task. She didn't want to put the blame solely on other teens, but Rory had been struggling so much more since hanging out with Truitt and Kai.

He'd been such a sweet kid, the first to share his cookie or pick a wildflower for her because he knew how much she loved them. These days, he couldn't even be bothered to pick up his own backpack off the stairs.

When she'd landed this job, she'd looked forward to all the ways this place fostered peace. Each event had a purpose beyond fun. Trail rides tapped into equine therapy. Thcy ingrained utilizing the five senses for grounding—making scented candles, singing with the ranch's Raise the Woof band or mixing potpourri from dried flowers grown locally. The ranch boasted its own hot springs in a cave. Packtivity offerings were endless.

The thought of how she could have lost her job over Rory's stunt made her stomach plummet.

Rosie gave a squeak and Charlotte realized she'd been holding her a bit too tightly. She eased her grip but still the furry scrap wriggled to get down.

"I'm so sorry, little one." She set the dog on the floor. Rosie scampered across the floor, painted nails clicking as she made her way to a dog bed by the fireplace. With an efficient hop onto the pink cushion, she curled up and began licking her paws. "Nap well. We'll play ball later. I promise."

Starting up the narrow stairway, she scooped up Rory's bag on her way up to the closed-in loft bedroom. It wasn't large, though the space had its own bathroom. Having him a floor above kept his mess out of sight—for the most part.

His backpack was heavy, heavier than normal, and she hated the suspicion stirring in her gut. She had to know… She tugged open the zipper and looked inside.

Books. Just books.

She breathed a sigh of relief and climbed the last step to the small landing.

"Rory?" she shouted over the throbbing beat of some song proclaiming how adults were the root of all evil. "Can you turn the music down?"

No response.

She tapped on the door, just below the sign that read: *Keep out. Gamer at play.* She'd grounded him from his game system last week, took the cord only to find out he had another one hidden for just such an occasion. With her brother, it felt like she was chasing her tail trying to come up with ways to keep him out of trouble and make him feel the consequences of his actions.

"Rory, open up. We have to talk before you go to school."

Thank goodness she could rest easy knowing where he was today while she sorted through the rest. Her chest went tight at the thought of facing her boss. Her family needed this job.

"Rory, I'm coming in—"

Before she could finish the sentence, he yanked open the door. Morning light filled his room, filtering through the gauzy white curtains. Gentle light contrasted with his furrowed brow and disheveled dirty blond hair. “Why didn’t you answer your phone?”

She blinked in surprise at the accusation. She wasn’t the one who’d committed a crime. “I must have been sleeping hard.” She thrust his backpack toward him. “So hard, after all, that I didn’t hear you sneak out.”

Rory fidgeted with the strings on his hoodie, feet practically dragging as he made his way to the green dresser, halfheartedly stuffing a notebook and calculator into his backpack. “I guess this means I’m grounded.”

Grounded? She slumped against the door frame. “You’re lucky you aren’t in jail.”

He cast her a side-eye, the green so like their mother’s, then looked away. “We were just messing around.”

“You broke into a store.” She could still hardly wrap her brain around it. “That’s against the law.”

“Stupid law. We didn’t take anything.” He yanked the zipper shut on his backpack.

“Vandalism is against the law, too. You destroyed property with graffiti. And you broke into the shop.” Her anger grew with each word. The act alone was bad enough, but why did he have to choose a business owned by her boss? “Do you have any idea how lucky you are not to be facing a harsher punishment? Jail time, even?”

“Go ahead, then. Ship me off.” His jaw jutted, full

of peach fuzz and defiance even as his voice trembled. "Your life will be easier without me."

At his hint of vulnerability, the fight seeped right out of her. Still, she had to stick to her guns with her brother. He was too good at sniffing out weakness.

"You know that's not going to happen. I'm not giving up on you. And neither are the other people in your life." She bent to scoop up frayed jeans and a stained T-shirt off the floor, tossing them in the laundry hamper. "Declan talked to Hollie and Jacob. They're willing to forgo pressing charges on one condition."

"What's that?" He kicked a sweatshirt and wadded-up socks toward the hamper.

She knew he was just trying to get a rise out of her. She was learning to choose her battles with her brother. "Your accomplices will be picking up trash and painting over the damage at the gift shop. You will muck out horse stalls."

"No wonder the O'Briens don't want to press charges. They're getting free help. Aren't there child labor laws in this country?" He raked a hand through his mussed hair.

Charlotte exhaled hard. Counted to ten. "You're incredibly lucky that they're being so forgiving. You're lucky in a lot of ways, and the sooner you realize that, the sooner you'll quit feeling so mad all the time."

"Fine. Sure. Whatever. Can I get changed for school?" Fresh clothes were uncharacteristically laid out on his unmade bed, covering the upturned red plaid duvet. Like he wanted out of here. Fast.

"Of course. I'll drive you."

Before he could argue, she walked out with the laundry basket, picking up that hoodie he'd attempted to put in there. She kicked the door closed behind her. She was running late already and she still needed to call Hollie O'Brien, and take Rory to school.

Right now, Charlotte sure didn't trust him to get on the bus. Or even walk in the building when the bus arrived.

This couldn't have happened at a worse time. She had a packed day ahead of her—a packed month, for that matter. She'd planned a massive spring May Day festival with all new landscaping. Morning, noon and often into the evening, she was planting and pruning and prepping. Good promo from the event would take her career to the next level.

All the more important with a baby on the way.

A whisper of guilt pinched. If she hadn't been so focused on work, if she'd been keeping better watch over Rory, maybe none of this would have happened. She'd been all too eager to use work as a diversion from the ache of her breakup.

This second chance for her brother was too important to screw up and time was running out. If Rory felt in the way now, she worried how he would react to the pregnancy.

And what about Declan's reaction when she told him? When would be the right time? She knew she couldn't keep it secret forever. Still, would it be so wrong to wait until things settled down with Rory and after the spring event? Then, she could focus solely on figuring out what, if any, role Declan would play in this child's life.

Mind made up, she started down the stairs for a shower and more crackers. With each step, she ignored the little voice insisting she was delaying to avoid having to deal with bringing Declan back into her life.

Declan's day had started early and would finish late.

But work was his life.

He put the cop cruiser into Park outside the dude ranch's main stable. He'd checked in at the gift shop and seen that Kai had already started painting the wall. Truitt was picking up trash around the campground.

Two down, one to go.

If Rory ditched? Then, Declan would have to take the teen down to the station. Declan rubbed the back of his neck over the pinch of tension at the possibility of bringing more stress to Charlotte's doorstep.

And if he ran into Charlotte today? Maybe he could dispel some of the tension between them. An apology would be one place to start. He knew he should have called her or texted. Or something. It wasn't her fault he was a jerk.

His duty boots hit the dusty earth and he jammed

his hat on his head, scanning the stable area humming with activity from guests to staff. The Top Dog Dude Ranch was quite a spread and growing by the minute. Nestled in the Smoky Mountains, the getaway had quickly become the go-to vacation spot.

To call it a resort was a disservice. The Top Dog Dude Ranch offered a back-to-nature experience in a way that went far behind aesthetics. This was a place to heal the heart and strengthen bonds. As a cop, he recognized the rehabilitative spirit the owners had woven into every element while protecting the beauty of the forest.

Cabins were nestled between trees. They even had vintage campers restored for glamping in a scenic campground near the hot springs. The main lodge sprawled, built from logs. The ranch had a little "Main Street" of sorts, all built with an old west vibe. A gift shop. A bakery and ice cream café.

A flower stand and greenhouse.

He pulled his mind off thoughts of Charlotte and pointed his boots toward the main barn. The ranch sported a stable with a small arena, along with two other barns. One for additional animals, another used for parties. All events were down-to-earth and family-oriented.

The air echoed with the huff of horses and wind rustling branches full of spring leaves, laughter threading through the breeze like confetti. He could have used a place like this when he was growing up. Not that his mom could have afforded a vacation here.

But man, he would have loved an after-school job in a similar setting.

Somewhere safe.

He couldn't change his past. But he could use it to help change things for others.

Charging ahead, he passed by two couples embarking on a hike, then a family leading their horses back from a trail ride. Finally, he spotted the ranch owner, Jacob O'Brien. The towering man was inspecting a horse's hoof, while his son Freddy sat on a split rail fence watching, feet swinging. The family dog, a collie named Ziggy, stayed near the boy, chocolate eyes not missing a beat. The dog was a tried-and-true farm dog, well versed in staying clear of hooves.

Waving, Declan called out, "O'Brien, how's it going?"

Jacob released the horse's leg and set him free into the grazing area with a light pat on the haunches. "Much better than I thought. I was checking on the healing of an abscess. Luckily, we've turned a corner. What can I do for you?"

Declan scratched Ziggy behind the ears, the collie leaning against his leg begging for more. "I'm just following up on the incident at the gift shop. Is our problem child here yet?"

As good an excuse as any for showing up. And certainly better than revealing how much he wanted to see the boy's sister. Something had been "off" with her earlier, something that seemed unrelated to the crisis with her brother. Declan couldn't put his finger on it, but the police officer in him just couldn't let the mystery go unsolved.

Jacob pulled out his cell phone. "According to Charlotte's text, they should be arriving any minute now. She went into town to pick him up from school rather than trust him getting on and off the bus."

"Smart lady." And busy. He knew she took pride in her job, so that trip to the high school meant she would have to work late. At least Rory would be on spring break soon. All the more reason to keep him busy in the stables.

Freddy leaned forward on the split rail, closer to the conversation. "Did Rory do something bad?"

"Well, son." Jacob clapped the boy on the shoulder. "He and his friends got in a spot of trouble. Now they're doing extra chores as a way of showing they're sorry."

Nodding, Freddy hopped down off the fence, facing Declan. "I used to get in a lot of trouble, too. I still do sometimes, but not as much. Right, Dad?"

Jacob ruffled his hair. "Absolutely right. I'm proud of how hard you're working at listening."

Some men were just cut out to be fathers. Declan also knew he wasn't one of them.

Freddy and his three siblings had gone into foster care after their parents died. Jacob and Hollie O'Brien had adopted all four to keep them together. Declan knew how tough it was to keep that many kids together. He'd seen more than his share of brothers and sisters separated during his own stints in and out of foster homes. "I can tell you're a great helper with your dad here."

"I'm trying," Freddy said, then pivoted hard to face Declan again. "Can I wear your hat?"

Jacob frowned. "That's his uniform—"

Declan interrupted, "No worries. I'm off duty." He swept his hat off and dropped it on Freddy's head. "Looks good, kiddo. You're not angling to take my job, now, are you?"

"Well, Sheriff Winslow," Freddy said with an impish gleam in his eyes. "You never know. Hey, Dad, can I show my friend Benji the hat? He's just right over there by the chickens. I promise I'll take good care of it."

Jacob nodded and Freddy took off running, hand on the hat to anchor it in place. Ziggy trotted alongside.

Once the boy was gone, Jacob hitched a booted foot on the bottom fence rail. Cricket, one of the quarter horses, angled toward the fence, excited to see the small group of people leaning over. "Sure glad you were the one to catch the call last night when the alarm went off," Jacob said.

"And I'm glad you were willing to work out a deal."

"Well, it helped that we caught the kids early on in the act before they inflicted too much damage. Just a few squiggly swirls in red paint on the whitewashed walls. Gwen—the gift shop manager—tacked a quilt over the graffiti first thing this morning so she could open up. That did the job well enough until the boys came to paint—"

Jacob stopped midsentence and nodded toward the narrow road leading past the main lodge to the stables. Charlotte's blue vintage truck jostled along, the shocks on the vehicle in questionable condition. She'd once told him the vintage pickup—named Myrtle—was more than just practical for her job, it also had sentimental value.

With her elbow hitched out the open window, she steered closer, her blond hair catching in the breeze. A long strand trailed out. Rory sat slouched in the passenger side. The old truck pulled up alongside his cop cruiser, Myrtle's brakes squealing. Charlotte threw it into Park and hopped out.

Declan adjusted his sunglasses, making the most of the chance to study her unnoticed, thanks to the shades. The baggy overalls with dirt on the knees signaled that she must have stopped some work project midway to hop in the truck. Her gardening Crocs were covered in mud, a faded daisy just barely peeking out.

And she looked gorgeous. The hint of sun kissing her cheeks as he'd once done. The scent of lavender and roses clinging to her.

Rory slammed the passenger door closed with far more force than necessary. "See, Sheriff, I'm here. If you're gonna check up on me all the time, you might as well give me an ankle monitor." He scuffed his gym shoes through the dirt as he strode toward Jacob. "Where do I start?"

A slow smile broke out on Jacob's face. "Follow me. You can begin with Goliath's stall. He had a big breakfast."

The two retreated, disappearing into the barn. Leaving Declan alone with Charlotte. Well, somewhat alone, given there were at last a couple of dozen ranch guests weaving around them.

He turned to Charlotte and found her covering her mouth, stifling a laugh. "I was going to ask you how you are holding up, but given your expression over Goliath's big breakfast, you seem okay."

Her hand fell away. "It feels good to laugh."

"It's been a rough day," Declan said, taking inventory again of the dark circles under her eyes.

"Truthfully, it's been a tough few months." She slumped back against the fence. "This may sound crazy, but as I was driving Rory back from school today, I felt relieved. As long as he's working here, I don't have to wonder where he is or what he's doing. And maybe he'll be so exhausted afterward, he will be too tired to sneak out in the middle of the night."

"That's the idea." He hooked his thumbs in his belt loops to keep from reaching for her. He'd given up that right. "I'm glad it could give you peace."

"For what it's worth, I'm not just dumping him off and expecting others to look after him." A flash of guilt stamped across her pale face, which held just a hint of pink from the sun on her cheeks.

"I never thought that for even a minute." And he hated that she'd considered it at all. "You've done more for him than any sister should have to take on." More than anyone in his family had been able to do for him. He hoped Rory appreciated how lucky he was—but Declan doubted it.

Charlotte traced the toe of her Croc in the dirt. "I changed the code on the security system. He doesn't have it. If he tries to leave in the middle of the night, I—and the whole ranch—will know about it."

Still, she didn't move to leave. And he couldn't will his feet to carry him away, either. He was playing with fire, standing here talking to her, sinking into the easy pleasure of just being near her. "Teens are tough, even under the best of circumstances."

"Thank you for stepping up to help with him." She crossed her arms over her chest, accentuating her breasts, fuller than he recalled. "Since our dad walked out, it's been hard for Rory, not growing up with a father figure."

"I can identify with that." Rustling through the wisps of hay behind them came Pippa, a gray tabby, followed closely by her littermate, an orange tabby named Porkchop. The two young cats ran full speed, leaping onto the fence railing with two soft thuds.

"I guess you can."

They'd shared the basics of their childhoods—she knew that he'd never known his dad and that his mom had struggled to make ends meet. But he'd told her nothing about foster care.

In turn, she'd told him about her mother's battle with depression and how her father walked out. Was there more to her story as well?

He and Charlotte had been so tangled up in the explosive chemistry between them, they hadn't done much talking. Not that he thought it would have changed how things ended, other than making it even tougher to say goodbye. He'd learned that lesson from zipping in and out of foster homes.

Silence descended as Pippa walked closer to him, winding around his legs. Clearing his throat, he began again, "Did you manage to snag a nap during your lunch break? You don't look as green as you did this morning."

"So you're saying that before, I looked green and exhausted? Gee thanks." She winced, but before he could apologize, she continued, "But yes, I'm feeling much better. I've been working all day, even ate lunch on the fly—barbecue from the ranch's kitchen. So good. I can't get enough of it these days—"

Biting her bottom lip, she stuffed her hands into the pockets of her baggy overalls, backing away so fast she nearly bumped into a group of teenage girls. "I should get back to work."

Her abrupt shift startled him, nudging his Spidey sense again that something was off. Maybe he was just looking for excuses to check in on her. Maybe not.

Either way, he didn't intend to let up until he put his mind at rest about whatever she was hiding.

* * *

Rory Pace hated his life.

He'd thought it was bad before, and now it sucked even worse, thanks to that stupid prank and everyone's totally over-the-top reaction. It wasn't like they were going to steal anything. It had all started because the gift shop manager—Ms. Bishop—wouldn't give Truitt a job. Then Ms. Bishop had followed them around, watching their every move whenever they came in.

So Kai decided they should spray some stuff on the wall. Harmless. Easy to fix.

But now, here Rory was, blisters forming on his hands beneath his leather gloves. The smell of the barns would be in his nostrils for days, the hay clinging to his clothes and making his back itch.

He couldn't believe he was shoveling out horse stables. His buddies got cakewalk jobs in comparison, which sucked since breaking in was their idea in the first place. Truitt, who'd bought the spray cans, was picking up trash at the campground and Kai, who'd planned the whole thing, was slapping some paint on the wall at the gift shop.

Supposedly they were doing some other stuff too, but he didn't believe it. They had parents and money and fancy lawyers to fall back on, so it was no wonder their jobs didn't involve blisters and hard labor. He just had a cranky sister and a crazy mother who was locked away in a hospital.

He knew his mom needed help, but couldn't she

have figured out a way to do one of those outpatient deals he'd read about? Where she did all her therapy stuff during the day but came home at night? But no, she'd *chosen* not to be there for him. The defection hurt.

And then Declan had to go MIA, too. Even though the guy had tried to fake like they were friends, like he actually gave a damn about Rory, back when the sheriff had been dating Charlotte.

Gripping the wooden handle of the stall-mucking rake, he scooped and sifted the horse poop. Rory dumped the waste into the wheelbarrow as giggles from an approaching group of high-school-aged girls snagged his attention. The trio of females were still at the far end of the stables, absorbed in their conversation. From their animated movements, it was safe to say they hadn't noticed him, even as they slowed to a stop just beyond his current stall.

Well, hello. Rory stabbed the shovel into the ground and leaned on the handle, taking in the view as he helped himself to a momentary and much-deserved break. The three of them had different styles, each one prettier than the next.

Listening, he caught their names. Zoey, he gathered from the snippets of conversation, was the one with deep red hair in perfect spirals. Long silver earrings framed her pale face. Corrine, the girl with short blond hair shaved shorter on one side, fiddled with her oversize vintage band T-shirt. The last girl, Olivia, captivated Rory's attention even more than the others. Her straight dark hair matched the richness of her brown eyes. Her leggings and tee bore a logo for a junior orchestra. He swallowed, hoping it wasn't audible.

Zoey scrolled on her phone as they stood in a semicircle. "Did you hear that Jade went on a cruise with her family?"

Olivia tucked her sleek black hair behind her ear. "She texted me that they all got seasick and are stuck in their staterooms."

Corrine rolled her eyes with a dramatic sweep of her overlong eyelashes. "Poor Jade. If you ask me, it serves her right for being such a snob about getting a cooler spring break."

"Maybe," Olivia said, shrugging her shoulders. "This place is better than I expected, especially since you're both here."

Zoey hooked arms with her two friends, leaning her head on Corrine's shoulder. "Thank goodness our parents rented the cabin together. What do you want to do now? Olivia, pull up the website on your phone."

"Or we can ask." For the first time since they had stopped walking, Olivia turned to face him. So she *had* seen him after all. "What's the best thing for teenagers to do around this place? Preferably, something that isn't full of old fogies."

Her deep brown eyes rooted him to the spot and made him wish he was wearing something other than horse dung. Yet another reason to be mad at his sister, the ranch and life in general. He'd already brought enough sweat to the stable job for the day, hadn't he?

Tossing aside the shovel, he peeled off the gloves. "Happy to help. How about I show you around?"

With a final pat on Goliath's nose, he stepped away from the stinky stall and straight toward the welcome distraction from living in this loser place.

Chapter Three

Usually Charlotte found her job calming, appreciating the cool earth, the scent of verdant growth. The timelessness of coaxing life from soil anchored her.

But not today.

Too much knocked around inside her, stealing the joy of work, so much work, to prepare for the ranch's May Day festival. She had to catch up on lost hours transporting Rory to and from school. With the spring extravaganza coming up in a couple of weeks, time was running out. And while she desperately needed to go home and eat, at least staying here sprucing up the main lodge's gardens kept her close to the stables where Rory was shoveling his way to redemption late into the afternoon.

A group of children gathered in a fenced-up petting zoo area. A father hefted up his daughter to feed carrots to a miniature pony. Two boys scattered seed to a pen of chickens. The little barnyard was alive with squeals and excitement as children interacted with a piglet, three sheep and two rabbits. In a neighboring fenced area, pony rides circled the enclosed space. Country music drifted from speakers mounted on the side of the barn. It was the perfect place for children... But she felt so unprepared to bring a child of her *own* into her life here.

Her heart squeezed with worry, wondering what the future held. For one thing, how involved would Declan be in his kid's life?

Her gaze zipped over to a small clearing where the object of her thoughts—Declan himself—stood leading a basics of self-defense class for ranch guests, especially for ladies who'd experienced trauma. Declan and a local counselor presented together, offering these people an opportunity for healing and empowerment. His shoulders broad and steady in his uniform. His whole presence broadcasting charismatic strength from his duty boots all the way up to his wide-brimmed hat.

Why did he have to be so perfect and so very wrong all at the same time?

With practiced fingers, she snipped some of the wild ginger and violets with gardening sheers, placing the clippings carefully in the hand-woven basket. She would dry these pieces to use in soaps and floral arrangements. She missed her little doggie helper, but Rosie was at the Top Dog's groomer.

Another perk of working at the ranch.

After a deep breath, she moved from the planter with the yellow lady's slippers toward one of the walking paths around the lodge. Kneeling, she adjusted the pink gardening gloves before gently waving aside a bee flitting from one flower to another. Working with a steadiness she did not feel, she uprooted weeds from the flower beds, letting the blue phlox and mountain laurel shine in the plant beds.

Charlotte made her way down the plant bed. She couldn't help but glance occasionally over her shoulder toward the barn, searching for Rory until finally, she found him. He looked dirty, sweaty and miserable. He hefted bales of hay, pieces falling haphazardly behind him as he wove around guests. A large family reunion was going for an evening wagon ride to the springs. A group of teenage girls on spring break strolled toward the bonfire area.

The latter was something Rory seemed to notice, given how his shoveling slowed until the girls merged into the crowd around the massive stone firepit.

Moving from the walking path to the gazebo in front of the barn, Charlotte sighed. Chewing the inside of her cheek, she submerged her gloved hands into the loamy soil.

Hollie emerged from the barn, wearing jeans, a

Top Dog T-shirt and a Stetson. Smiling, she waved. "Hey there. Are you still at it?"

"I'm just doing my job."

"Trust me, we're getting more than our money's worth with you." Hollie dropped to sit on a stack of wooden pallets, her boots dusty. "It would have been alright for you to take the rest of the day off. I know you've been awake since early and you drove Rory into school."

"I take pride in my work." Charlotte held up one of her clippings—mountain laurel—with a small smile. The mountain laurel bar soap already proved to be one of her most popular artisan soaps. "I won't let you down."

"You put in far more hours than is in your contract." Hollie leveled an honest, serious gaze her way. "Your job is not in jeopardy. I promise."

Charlotte patted the fresh potting soil around a large flame azalea in a rustic brown pot, her stomach in knots, a combination of her pregnancy and nerves. "I'm sorry for Rory's attitude. You've been so gracious and he should apologize."

"He's here and working hard." Hollie put her hand over Charlotte's, stilling the frenetic busyness. "That's a step in the right direction."

"Thank you for giving him this chance." Sighing, heart weary, Charlotte moved aside a spade and trowel, then sank back to sit. "He wasn't always this way. I don't want to make excuses for him, but he has had a rough time of it. Maybe this is what he needs to straighten himself out. Please just know I'm grateful and will not take my eyes off him."

"You're an incredible asset to the ranch. We know that. Nobody here thinks less of you because of what your brother did. And truthfully, I believe Rory's worth the investment of a second chance." Hollie smiled sympathetically. "I know a thing or two about misunderstood boys after the rocky start we had with Freddy."

Charlotte blinked back tears that seemed all too close to the surface these days. Hormones, perhaps? Her throat grew tight as she reached for the worry stone in the left pocket of her apron. Always centering herself through the gifts of nature. "I appreciate that."

"Our ranch is all about second chances." Hollie adjusted the brim of her hat as the sun beat down, casting her face in shadows. "Since you've had a long day, how about joining Jacob and me for supper? Our kitchen is quiet, we can visit."

That sounded wonderful, to have a normal evening with a friend and pretend her life wasn't falling down around her ears. Wonderful—and not possible. Not tonight anyway. "That's kind of you, but I don't want to intrude… And, of course, there's Rory to consider."

"Well," Hollie said with a wink, "I have it on good authority he will be working very late."

A much-needed laugh whispered free, along with relief. She patted the soil around the flame azalea, pouring a bit of water from the watering can onto the repotted plant. "Hopefully he'll be too worn out to pay attention to the teenage girls hanging out around the barn."

"Is a teenage boy ever that tired?" Hollie said with a grin. "But don't worry. The stable manager knows to keep a close watch over him."

It felt good to have help with her brother. Shouldering the challenge of caring for a troubled teen alone was harder than she'd expected. Her gaze wandered back to Declan as she thought of how he'd handled her brother this morning, with calm and confidence.

He would make a good father. He was such a man of honor, she didn't expect him to walk away from his child. But would he be glad about the baby or would he see fatherhood as a burden?

See *her* as a burden?

Her chest went tight with anxiety. She needed to step away from the sight of him. Fast. "Well, okay, then."

"Good, it's a plan, then." Hollie shoved to her feet, dusting her fingers along her jeans before raising her hands to her mouth and shouting, "Declan? Would you like to join us for supper?"

Declan appreciated a home-cooked meal as much as the next fellow. In fact, the offer of barbecue and cobbler might well be considered his kryptonite.

But he had to wonder if his friend Hollie had known that when inviting him to dinner tonight in what looked suspiciously like a double date. He hadn't realized the O'Brien kids would be off at some ranch pack-tivity.

He should have said no to the dinner invitation. And yet, one glance at Charlotte looking all sweaty and wilted and undeniably beautiful had him saying yes.

Now here he sat in the O'Briens' kitchen, at their huge oak table, with Hollie, Jacob and Charlotte, polishing off the last of their berry cobbler while they talked. And he listened, their voices warming the air with a sense of community he knew was rare.

Draining his glass of sweet tea, he allowed himself a moment to drink in the sight of Charlotte. She sure didn't look messy now. She'd swapped out of her overalls into a clean pair of jeans and a long Top Dog T-shirt. He knew from their time together that she kept a change of clothes in her greenhouse office in case she needed to meet with guests. Her blond, sun-streaked hair was swept back with a flowered headband.

She smelled of earth and lavender, a scent that sometimes haunted his dreams with memories of their time together. So brief. But undeniably memorable.

"Declan?" Jacob's voice cut through his thoughts.

"Yeah? Sorry. I was thinking about work tomorrow." He blinked, adjusting back to the present moment and the dimmed, warm overhead lighting.

Hollie leaned forward on the oak table. "Sounds

like you need a vacation at the Top Dog Dude Ranch to decompress."

"I wouldn't mind that one bit." The kitchen showcased the healing vibe of the ranch along with the O'Briens' love of animals. Arranged in gallery walls, paw prints, dog portraits and dog-themed plaques were gathered—a representation of decades of joint collecting. "Home is where the dog is." "Love is a four-legged word." "Live, Love, Bark."

"Looks like you've added a few new signs." His head tilted toward the gallery wall.

Hollie turned toward Jacob, a gleam in her bright eyes meant just for her husband. "I have to confess to being somewhat addicted to collecting them. Jacob even brought one back as a present for our third anniversary when he traveled to purchase six horses. Wasn't that romantic?"

At the word *romantic*, Charlotte shot to her feet and put her plate on the black-and-white granite countertops, then took her time refilling her sweet tea. "Yes, totally. And they make for a fun vibe to your kitchen decor."

Jacob grinned, eyes darting around the room. "We have a number of kitchen spaces throughout the ranch, given how much entertaining happens, but this one is our favorite."

Laughing, Hollie untwined a strand of hair from her silver hoop earring. "You should have seen it the night our freezer went out right before a massive spring wedding. We were rushing around baking up all the contents as quickly as we could so that as little as possible went to waste."

Jacob reached to clasp his wife's hand, squeezing. "Hollie was really quick on her feet rethinking menus that had been planned out for weeks. She's amazing."

Their love for each other was palpable. And from all he'd heard, theirs hadn't been an easy path. Hollie's cancer battle. Infertility. Adopting an infant only to have the birth mother change her mind.

Yet, through it all, here they were, with a rock-solid marriage, four beautiful children and a thriving business. So much joy.

And so much to risk losing. Declan was content with his life. He had a job he loved and a place in this community. It was enough. It had to be. "Thanks for including me."

"Our pleasure," Hollie said. "When the kids said they wanted to hang out with their friends for movie night, it seemed only fair that we get to have an evening with our friends as well."

Declan turned his cup on the table. "It's quite a perk for staff to be able to use the pack-tivities as well. Like a permanent vacation."

Charlotte took her tea and sat on one of the tree trunk barstools near the table. "And you have such a great variety of options, especially when it comes to entertaining the kids in a way that's more than just childcare."

Hollie's thumb stroked over Jacob's fingers. "We

have our own little event consultants here in-house. They have ideas for us all the time. Right, Jacob?"

"Some more workable than others." Jacob's mouth quirked in a half smile. "Phillip wanted us to put in a water park. We had to explain to him about protecting the integrity of the natural look of the land."

Hollie leaned back in her chair laughing. "Next thing we knew, he'd drawn a whole proposal of how it could fit into a mountainside. He vowed—and I quote—'Miss Charlotte will make it beautiful. She makes everything pretty.'"

With a grimace of embarrassment, Charlotte clasped her hands together. "You're going to make me blush. I'll have to give that kid a treat next time I see him."

"We finally managed to talk him out of the idea—and now we're trying to get him excited about our latest plan," Hollie said, dabbing a napkin to the corner of her mouth. "We're working on expanding the offerings to the guests to increase our infant and toddler childcare."

Charlotte choked on a swallow of tea, covered her mouth with a napkin and waved aside concern. "I'm okay. Go ahead."

"Well," Hollie continued, "our stable manager, Eliza, has those two little ones underfoot now that she's engaged to Doc Barnett. And our newest kitchen hire is pregnant. All these babies and toddlers got us brainstorming possibilities for guests as well as staff. In particular, how can we help someone struggling with postpartum depression?" Her eyes filled with shadows.

Jacob took her hand again and filled in the awkward silence. "We're still in the planning stages, but we're considering everything from indulge-her packages for the new mom, to on-site nannies who wouldn't just do drop-off babysitting, but could also accompany the family so the new parents could have an extra set of hands with the little ones."

"We're working on sponsorships from former guests to pay for 'gift packages' to families who might not otherwise be able to afford the extra service."

Jacob scooped up another bite of berry cobbler. "But enough talking shop. Declan, tell us about your Guard duty. Did you go somewhere exciting? Or dangerous? Or is it secret?"

Declan scratched behind his ear. Not a secret at all and not nearly as dangerous or exciting as they appeared to think. "My Guard duty wasn't tough in the traditional sense."

Hollie leaned forward, elbows on the edge of the table. "What happened?"

Grinning, Declan sat back in his chair. "You're all gonna laugh."

Charlotte shook her head.

Jacob said, "Not a chance."

Hollie assured, "Cross my heart."

"I was sent to fill in the gaps for a school in an underserved district," he said, watching Charlotte's face for her reaction. Her forehead crinkled in confusion, then hurt.

Had she worried about him, assuming he might be on a dangerous assignment? Did she think that was why he hadn't been in touch? He'd just figured she wouldn't want to hear from him. Their break had been quick and complete.

And, yes, painful.

Hollie clapped a hand over her mouth. "You were a substitute teacher? I'm not laughing. I promise. I just don't think of that for Guard duty."

Neither had he. "There was a severe teacher shortage in a few small towns out west. We were called up to fill the gap for three months. I was glad to help, to make a difference."

Jacob lifted his glass of tea. "What subject did you 'teach'?"

"High school civics and history," Declan said dryly, thumbing the edge of his glass.

"Civics? What a great fit and use of your experience in law enforcement. I bet they learned so much."

"I don't know about that. I think I was chosen more to keep them from killing each other." He paused, gathering his thoughts before he shared something he didn't intend. Something about this family-style gathering had lowered his defenses. "That came out harsher than I intended. Forget I said anything."

Hollie folded her cloth napkin and set it aside.

"You don't have to talk if you would rather not. I can see it wasn't, uh, a pleasant tour of duty."

Weighing his words, he tried to locate a midground. "I'm glad I was able to help, and it wasn't all bad. But there were plenty of reminders of my own youth. It brought back some bad memories."

His days had been filled with kids making one bad decision after another.

"I'm sorry to hear that."

"In some ways, it helps me to remember where I came from. It offers me a way to give back in honor of those who helped me." Truth. A truth that also made him uncomfortable, needing to be anywhere but in the middle of this conversation. "Well, folks, thank you for a great dinner, but I need to head back over to the stable to get my car."

As he started to stand, Charlotte rested a hand on his arm, stopping him cold. Her touch unexpected.

And missed.

Her blue eyes serious, she said, "I imagine it's time to get Rory. Mind if I tag along?"

Charlotte was fast realizing she needed to tell Declan about the pregnancy soon. The longer she waited, the more awkward it would be, running into him regularly and keeping her secret. Truth be told, she couldn't stomach the thought of the stress of having it hanging over her head.

So she'd asked to walk with him.

Cool air rushed toward them as they strolled out

through the O'Brien's private patio. The last rays of light retreated, washing the sky in blue-violet as stars winked on the scene overhead. She navigated her way past wildflowers planted in carefully constructed chaos, a design Charlotte was particularly proud of. Shortly after coming here to work, she'd created a "sniff garden" safe for their many roaming animals. The area surrounding the base of the trees was overflowing with airy dill, aromatic rosemary, leafy clusters of purple basil, a small sea of catnip, blankets of deep green ferns. The occasional topiary gave the space a hint of order, anchoring the flow of the rest.

Charlotte understood how important animals were to the O'Briens and had taken great care to create a bin for dog toys as well as an elaborate, multilevel cat climbing tower. Two overstuffed lounge chairs huddled near the stone firepit, already primed with a tower of wood.

It was only a hundred yards or so to the stable, a brief distance really, but safe from temptation in that there were people milling all around them as they left the patio. Guests walking to their cabin, people relaxed and happy. She was glad for them—honored to be a part of making that happen.

And she was envious. What she wouldn't give to feel relaxed, for a change,

Dinner, at first, had been easier than she expected. Too easy. Like two couples on a normal double date with a night away from the kids. Except they weren't a couple. Not anymore. Now, it was time to move forward into their complicated future together.

Charlotte picked at her fingernails. "I'm sorry Hollie roped you into supper. Please know I didn't prompt her. I understand that we are over. Completely."

"Hollie means well. I'm aware the invitation was her idea." Declan scrubbed the back of his neck. "I hate that things are this awkward between us."

Her lips pressed together in a thin line as she searched for a way to ease the tension before she shared her news. "Hollie sure loaded you up with leftovers."

"I've been helping myself to the ranch's buffets so often, it probably seems like I'm taking advantage."

"I'm sure they don't see it that way. I know they're glad to have you back leading the self-defense class, and at no cost." She admired his generous spirit, reflected in so many of his actions. Such as how he'd gone the extra mile for Rory. "It makes sense you should eat while you're here."

"It's definitely preferable to cooking after working all day." Declan held up his doggy bag. "Did you get any rest? You seem bone-tired."

Did he have to keep reminding her how crummy she looked?

"I'm fine." She crossed her arms over her chest. "If anyone should be exhausted, it's you. Given you only just returned." From the trip he hadn't bothered to tell her about.

Her boots padded along the patio deck before she stopped to open the gate. She led them out toward the stables, walking beneath a small canopy of trees along one of her yet-to-be-weeded walking paths. An owl looked down at them from an oak tree. Inhaling the scent of spring air, she paused by a cluster of mountain laurel to pluck a weed from between the pink blossoms.

He stuffed his hands in his pockets, waiting. "You're mad that I didn't tell you where I went."

Yes. But she knew she shouldn't be. "We broke up. I had no right to know." They hadn't been tied to each other. Then. Now, they had a child together. She clenched her fist around the weed and charged ahead, focus set on the barn fifty yards ahead.

"But you're angry." He cast a sideways glance her way, his hat shading his eyes. "I can see it in your face. I understand you too well."

If he knew her that well, then he would realize she'd been worried, envisioning him somewhere in harm's way. Wondering if her baby would get to know his or her father.

"I'm frustrated. And yes, I'm tired. I'm also mad at myself for sleeping so hard that I missed my brother sneaking out. I won't make that mistake again."

"You have to know that if he wants to leave," he said gently, his brown eyes full of compassion, "then there's nothing you'll be able to do to stop him."

Her knees went weak and she sagged against a fat tree trunk. "Then what was the point of all this?"

"To buy some time to work with him in hopes he sees a better path for himself." Declan stopped walking, touched the side of her arm. Suddenly, the air evacuated her lungs as she met his gaze. "Regardless of how things shook out between you and me, I like the kid. I believe he has a shot, and I want to help him. If you'll let me."

As if things weren't already complicated enough between them. Still, it was her brother. Her baby brother who'd lost his home, who only got to see his mother on visiting days at a mental health facility—when their mom would even allow it. Most times, their mom canceled at the last minute.

The boy's life sucked.

Dragging in a deep breath, she nodded. "I don't know that I'm in a position to turn down help. Clearly, handling it on my own isn't working."

"Thank you." He skimmed back a stray strand of hair from her cheek and tucked it behind her ear. "I know that wasn't easy."

His touch sent a lovely shiver through her. Something she shouldn't be thinking about when she needed to find a way to tell him about the baby. Easier to talk about Rory when her brother's problems were very much on her mind. "I just don't know why you're so determined to do this."

His arm fell to his side. "Maybe it's my own way to make up for the rotten way things ended between us. You're a good person who deserved much better. I need to know you're okay."

"You want a clear conscience to walk away for good." She couldn't keep the bitter note from her voice.

"Maybe," he said hoarsely, his gaze holding hers.

Breathing in the spicy scent of him, she ached to lean against his muscular chest and let him help shoulder her worries. Such a dangerous, selfish thought. She needed to think about her brother and her baby.

She pushed away from the tree. Fast. Too fast.

The world tilted, then narrowed as she felt herself losing consciousness.

Chapter Four

Declan had dreamed of having Charlotte in his arms again, but not this way. The worry knotting his gut as he caught her limp body threatened his every professional instinct.

He cradled her against his chest as he knelt to the ground, only somewhat reassured by the steady rise and fall of her chest. He was used to reacting fast in a crisis. All a part of his job as a police officer and in the Guard.

Right now? This felt far too personal.

"Charlotte? Charlotte, honey, wake up," he said as he snatched his phone from his pocket to call for help. Hopefully, she would wake up before anyone had time to arrive, but someone should check her over, either way. He activated the screen, pulling up

Jacob's number. It was a long way to town and the ranch kept a nurse on staff.

And if an ambulance was needed?

Then he would load her in his car, along with the nurse, and turn on the siren. He would get to Moonlight Ridge faster than EMS could make the round trip here and back to town.

His heart hammered as fast and loudly as the bass music from a mini-rodeo in the arena. It seemed nightmarish and absurd that life was going on around him as if nothing was wrong.

The cell rang twice before Jacob answered. "Hey, buddy. Everything okay? Did you forget your doggy bag of leftovers?"

The bag of food lay on the ground, spilling open in a muddled mess of barbecue and berry cobbler from a meal that seemed to have happened a lifetime ago. "Charlotte fainted. Can you send the nurse? We're outside the stables."

As he spoke, one of the guests noticed them on the ground, a young woman who hovered close, concern in her eyes.

"Of course," Jacob answered him curtly, all business. "On our way."

The line disconnected.

A crowd was starting to gather, but already Charlotte was beginning to stir. Seeing her eyelashes flutter open helped him breathe easier. "Declan?"

Relief dulled the darker shades of panic. "Yeah, I'm here. Just stay still. Help is on the way."

"Help?" she asked, pushing up on one elbow.

"Whoa, whoa, hold on there. No need to jump up." He tightened his grip on her, supporting her back. "Jacob and Hollie are coming over with medical help. The ranch's nurse, I think. I was going to call 9-1-1, but if you need a hospital, it will be faster to take my car—"

"Excuse me," Jacob said as he shouldered his way through the onlookers.

Angling through the crowd, Jacob and Hollie rushed toward them, followed by Nolan Barnett, the small-town doctor engaged to Eliza, the ranch's stable manager. Charlotte would be in good hands.

The doctor was in his forties, dark hair and hints of silver hinting at years of wisdom and experience. Life had been tough on him with the death of his wife, then his son. Now he had custody of his two young grandchildren. He'd relocated to Moonlight Ridge for a slower pace to care for the kids.

The town was lucky to have him.

"Hey, Charlotte, how are you feeling?" The doctor took her pulse and checked her pupils, his air professional.

Charlotte swept a shaky hand along her hair, "Woozy, but okay. Really, I probably just didn't hydrate well enough out in the sun today."

"You didn't hit your head recently?"

"No, not at all." She elbowed herself upward.

"Skipping meals?" The doctor motioned toward

the remains of their doggy bag on the ground. "It looks like you haven't had supper yet."

Declan shook his head. "We just had a full meal with the O'Briens. They sent us home with extra."

"That sounds like Hollie and Jacob." Nolan pushed to his feet and held out a hand to help Charlotte stand.

Which she did. No swaying even though that didn't stop Declan from reaching out to steady her. "I'm good. Really."

Nolan eyed her for a moment before saying, "If you're sure. But I would still feel better if you stopped by the office for a checkup tomorrow."

"I'll call," she answered vaguely, her eyes darting away.

Declan had too many years on the force reading evasive individuals to miss the signs. What was she hiding? A thought to tuck away for later. Right now, he needed to make sure she was alright. "Charlotte—"

"I'm okay." She rested a hand on his arm, her touch light and familiar. "I need to get my brother, sooner rather than later, before he lands in more trouble."

Following the line of her gaze, he found the boy lounging against the side of the barn—flirting with a dark-haired girl in black leggings, clearly oblivious to what was going on with Charlotte. Declan sighed. He knew all too well how fast a female could make a guy lose his way.

Definitely time for the boy—and for Declan—to go.

* * *

The next day, Charlotte threw herself into work in her greenhouse, leading her favorite class—arranging dried flowers. Embracing routine, she shared information with the participants about all the health benefits of various plants. Roses and aloe vera were helpful for burns. Echinacea for the immune system. Hibiscus as an antioxidant. Lavender and primrose for stress and relaxation.

And speaking of Primrose, little Rosie napped on her dog bed under the table, looking too cute with her fresh grooming trim and new paisley bows on both her ears.

Charlotte waved as the class filed out, each participant leaving with an original arrangement.

"Thank you for coming," she said, gesturing toward a basket of favors on a plant stand by the door. "Don't forget your packets of seeds—your choice of lavender or English ivy. The instructions for germination are attached. Plants are more than pretty to look at. They also help purify the air in a home."

As the last ranch patron left, Charlotte shut the greenhouse door and flipped the sign to Closed, grateful for the peace. Even though it was her favorite class—usually—today it had felt like a chore. With each moment that ticked by, she felt more and more like a hypocrite for preaching on how to bring peace and harmony to life. She had a house full of all the best plants, and yet her world was total chaos.

With restless hands, she tucked bottles of homemade bubble bath for children into a slotted tray—

scented with flowers from her garden and made with eco-friendly ingredients. If only her life was as easily lined up.

All her plans to set things to rights by telling Declan about the pregnancy had been derailed by her fainting spell, which had scared her more than she wanted to let on. She'd checked in with her ob-gyn as soon as she'd gotten home, booking an appointment for that morning. Everything checked out fine. She'd been advised to get more rest.

Difficult to do when so much worry and responsibility weighed on her. Everywhere she looked these days, she saw something bringing a memory of Declan—the greenhouse more than anywhere, since they met here so often. Back when things seemed easy, uncomplicated, full of joy and passion.

Sighing, she braced a hand on the worktable and sank to the floor by Rosie. Threading her fingers through the little mutt's silky fur, Charlotte let the memories overtake her…

The greenhouse. Her haven. A landscaper's dream space.

Grow lights hummed overhead, casting a warm glow over rows of flowers and greenery, from lilacs to ferns. From hanging baskets along the rafters to pots in stands. Bundles of drying herbs and blooms hung upside down from hooks.

The scent of earth and plant life soothed her spirit and stirred her creativity.

She made fast tracks past a fountain that gurgled, made of a rustic pump flowing into an overlarge bucket. Angling by a stack of bagged soil. Finally, she pushed open the screen door separating her office from the main space. Behind her cluttered desk, the wall was full of sketches and plans for future landscape designs at the ranch. Warmth radiated outward as the door swung wide. She blinked, eyes adjusting to the dimmer lighting from the lone window.

Slipping inside, she closed the screen, then pulled the privacy curtain. Heart thudding wildly. Finally, she could snatch a moment just for herself and feed her craving.

Steely strong arms banded around her and pressed her to the desk.

"Hello, beautiful," Declan Winslow growled against her neck. "What took you so long?"

"Does it matter?" she whispered, breathing in the musky scent of his aftershave and gripping the crisp fabric of his uniform.

He was so handsome, her teeth hurt. And for now, he was hers.

His mouth found hers, fervent, familiar. Their relationship was only weeks old, but exciting. New. Just for her, a haven of happiness at a time of such stress in her life. She gobbled every moment with him.

His broad palms cradled her face as he kissed her and she kissed him right back, savoring the taste of coffee and him. She melted into the feel of him, enjoying the thrill of being in a new relationship, the butterflies, the spontaneity.

Charlotte eased back, her forehead resting against his. Inhaling deep, she drew in the scent of lavender and bergamot, two of the oils that she'd been working with last. "I'm glad you could make it here today. Sorry you had to hang out for so long."

"I'm glad I had the morning free, no emergencies. I enjoy this place. It's full of good people." He stroked a finger down the length of her braid. "Like you."

They'd met when he began doing security for larger events at Top Dog. Not that anything untoward had happened here. But the ranch prided itself on ensuring everyone's safety and he'd been willing to step into the need. He'd brushed aside any thanks from the O'Briens, saying that he was looking for something to fill his free time between work and the occasional National Guard Reserve duty.

She wondered sometimes if the man ever slept—and she had to admit she would like to watch him sleep. But she couldn't afford to leave her teenage brother unsupervised that long. The last time she'd stayed out past midnight, Rory had hosted a party at her cabin with over twenty "friends." Her boss had called her, concerned about the noise complaint. Keeping track of Rory was harder than she'd expected, but he didn't have anyone else after their mom's mental health deteriorated. There was no telling how long her mother would need treatment.

And Charlotte worried that even when released, her mom wouldn't be up to the challenge of looking after Rory.

Sighing, she flattened her palms to Declan's hard, muscled chest. "I should get back to work." She patted just over his thudding heart. "Rory can answer basic questions at my booth, but I imagine he's getting antsy. He was not happy about rolling out of bed so early this morning."

"Hold on for just a moment longer." Declan clasped her hands in his, his angular face somber. "Do you know where Rory was last night?"

A tap on the arm pulled Charlotte back to the present. She didn't mind at all since her memories had taken a dark turn.

Blinking away the fog, she found Gwen Bishop, the gift shop manager.

How could she have forgotten that Gwen would be coming by to pick up items for the shop? "Hello, Gwen. I didn't hear you knock. I must have been daydreaming."

Gwen smiled brightly, her blue eyes crinkling. Bright red hair framed her face in gentle waves. Like Charlotte, Gwen was a creative—she could pull together a display that transported people from the normal experience. She held her hand to her chest, toying with her necklace that had three little boy charms.

"Daydreaming is good for the spirit."

"I couldn't agree more." Charlotte motioned to the various crafts made with dried flowers—suncatchers, wreaths, shadow boxes, stationery with tiny petals and leaves pressed into the paper. "Let me help you load up."

"Thanks, I would really appreciate that. The triplets finish preschool in an hour and I have to pick them up. The life of a single mom," she said with a shrug.

Charlotte felt petty for being worried about her own life. And she hated even more what her brother had done, causing grief in this woman's life. "Thank you for what you did for my brother, cutting him a break."

"No thanks necessary." Gwen picked up a box labeled Sweet Dreams Bubble Bath. It was, admittedly, one of Charlotte's best batches yet. She infused Earl Grey tea, citrus oil and lavender into the bubble bath for a truly indulgent and skin-nourishing experience. "I understand he's had a difficult time with the move and changing schools. It can be tough finding the right crowd to hang out with it."

Carefully, Charlotte started to stack primrose soaps into a box, then grabbed a bag full of suncatchers before following Gwen to her minivan. "It goes deeper than that." She searched for the words, pulling them up even knowing it would be like coughing up shards of glass. As hard as it would be to share, Gwen deserved to know the full picture. "Our mother is bipolar. Deeply so. Her condition went untreated for decades, and with every manic-depressive episode, the next swing happened sooner with greater extremes. I got her into a good treatment facility. She's tried step-down programs but so far with no luck."

Gwen placed the boxes of bubble bath into the back of her minivan. Her brow crinkled in confusion as she leaned against the rear bumper. "And that's how you ended up with custody of your brother? I thought your parents were dead."

Her chest went tight. "Does that make you regret giving him the second chance to make amends?"

"Of course not." Gwen's eyes went wide, earnest, full of compassion. "Why would you think that?"

"Maybe you made your decision because you felt sorry for the orphan? Except he's not one." Her brother was just a deeply troubled teen whom she worried daily might need professional help.

"I made my decision because I can see that he's just a kid who's had a rough time."

"How can you be sure?" Charlotte asked on their way back into the greenhouse for the wreaths.

Taking a stack in her arms, Gwen nodded gently. "I recall this one particular time when the day ran long and my sons were tired of playing in the back room of the shop. They wanted to be outside in the snow like their friends."

Gwen continued as she walked back toward her minivan, "Rory offered to take them out for a snowball fight, right in front of the shop window so I could still see them. I know that may seem small to some. But to my boys and me? It meant the world. Rory's a good kid. I suspect he's just going to need a lot of support for a while."

Charlotte blinked back tears, needing that reassurance more than she'd realized. "Thank you for sharing that."

"Of course," Gwen said with a wink, stowing the last of the crafts and closing the back hatch. "I imagine you could do with some help as well. You're carrying a lot on your shoulders."

"I have a roof over my head, a job I love." She said it more to remind herself than to make a point.

"And Declan?" Gwen asked knowingly.

An all-too-familiar lump formed in her throat. Inhaling through her nose, and exhaling, Charlotte forced calm into her voice "We broke up. Remember?"

Gwen answered with silence.

"What?"

"Maybe I'm wrong." Gwen glanced over at her, forehead furrowed. "I thought…that you're pregnant."

Surprise rippled through Charlotte, then relief that finally, she could confide in someone. "Yes. But I haven't told anyone yet. I'm not going to be able to keep it a secret much longer. How did you guess?"

"You're glowing."

Charlotte huffed a strand of hair off her forehead. "I thought I look exhausted and green."

"Well, maybe a little," Gwen teased, crinkling her nose. "But that will fade right about the time you need to start sharing your news. Have you told Declan?"

"I was hoping to make it through the May Day festival, with all the floral preparation. Silly, maybe. It just seemed easier to wrap my head around talking it out with him once I have less on my plate."

Gwen drew her into a hug, and man, it felt good to have a friend right now, even if only to lean on for a moment. But all too soon that moment was cut short by a cop cruiser jostling up the path.

A cop car with a sheriff's seal on the door.

Gwen gave a quick wink and wave. "I need to get going. Good luck."

The single mom of three climbed behind the wheel of her minivan and drove down the oak-shaded path, leaving a cloud of dust behind.

Bracing herself for the inevitable draw she felt to Declan anytime he crossed her path, she turned to face him. Sheesh, he looked too good in that sheriff's uniform with the late day sun casting beams all around him.

As if she needed help noticing him. "What are you doing here? Is something wrong?"

"Nope. I had to stop by for a call on a missing hiker—already found by the time I arrived. I figured I would pick up Rory while I was here, drive you both back. I know you can walk, but it's been a long day." He kept right on taking charge in that slow-talking but immovable way of his. "I don't see Myrtle. You can both ride with me. Are you ready to go?"

While she'd agreed to his help the day before, this still felt, well, a little presumptuous. Sorta thoughtful, but mixed up with assumption. Irritation zipped through her. But she also didn't want to pick a fight, which would only make telling him about the baby more difficult.

In spite of all her best intentions to tell him right away, she just didn't have the energy for such a big discussion at the moment. Especially not with Rory nearby. She needed to come up with a plan.

And she needed to get home. She'd walked from her cabin to the greenhouse, trying to be healthy. "Alright. And thank you. Hold on while I get Rosie and lock the greenhouse."

She made quick work of putting the leftover and broken dried flowers in a bag to make potpourri sacks at home, then scooped up her dog under her arm like a football and headed back to the cruiser.

Where her brother waited in all his surly glory in the back seat.

Coughing, Rory pinched his nostrils shut. "It smells like a funeral parlor back here. Can't you stuff those in the trunk?"

Really? Her brother still didn't get that he should

tread warily after all he'd done? Charlotte drew in a deep breath. Counting to ten. Twice.

With a quick shake of the head, Declan glanced in the rearview mirror. "No room back there. I've got gear for work. You're welcome to walk beside the car if it bothers you that much."

"Not. Funny." Rory crossed his arms in a huff, slumping farther into the seat. "Besides, I'm too tired and sweaty."

"Rory—" Charlotte started.

Declan waved her silent and started the ignition. "Well, then the flowers will keep you from stinking up the car."

Securing her seat belt, Charlotte stifled a laugh and smiled her thanks. She forgot sometimes that Declan had a dry sense of humor. All the more amusing for how it crept out at unexpected moments. Tempting her with what could have been.

If only he hadn't broken her heart.

After a quiet ride to Charlotte's cabin, Declan pulled up on the dirt parking area beside her vintage truck, searching for a reason to keep Charlotte from walking away. His excuse for coming to the ranch had been made up. He'd come to check on her, but he wasn't any closer to settling the uneasy feeling he had about Charlotte.

Rory thumped the back of the seat. "Open the door, okay? I need a shower."

Charlotte twisted in her seat, startling little Rosie

snoozing in her lap. "Rory, how about you thank Declan for the ride?"

Declan shook his head. "We're good."

Pushing the boy would only set him off. Declan let him out of the car and the teen raced up the cabin steps. He paused only long enough for Charlotte to disarm the alarm using her phone and then Rory disappeared inside.

Declan pulled her pink duffel with embroidered daisies out of the car, slinging it over his shoulder while Charlotte opened her car door to let her little dog out. The fluffball bolted in a blink of an eye, darting around the yard, sniffing for the perfect spot.

Talking in low tones to her dog, Charlotte looked too pretty with her heat-flushed cheeks and her long legs showcased in jeans. He'd always been drawn to her down-to-earth style, from the simple headband to her high-top gym shoes. No Crocs today.

Declan maneuvered up the front stairs to set the bag down on the porch, then leaned against a post. "Do you have a minute to sit and talk?"

She looked back at the cabin, then at him again. Nodding, she sat on the top step. "Rosie could probably do with a little longer in the yard."

"You didn't answer my calls today." He sank down to sit beside her.

"I had a full schedule, most of which included teaching classes." She rubbed her hands along her well-worn jeans, the gesture relaying too clearly her nerves around him. "My phone was off."

"Did you make an appointment to see Doc Barnett?" He had to know. He'd been worried.

"I checked in with my own doctor," she said, avoiding his eyes. "I'm fine."

"People don't just pass out for no reason." He crossed his arms over his chest.

"I'm fine," she repeated, then turned to meet his gaze square-on, her blue eyes curious and a little confused. "Is that why you came by to pick up Rory today? So I would have to speak with you?"

"Yes."

"*Now* you want to talk?" she asked, her husky voice full of exasperation.

Tension crept up his neck. "I've apologized for not calling after I left town—"

"Actually, you haven't apologized." Her mouth went tight and thin for moment before she continued, "You explained your reasons, but the word *sorry* never crossed your lips."

Shc was right. He couldn't deny it.

Declan swallowed down the regret over having let her down in yet another way. "Then let me correct that. I apologize for not letting you know I wasn't in a war zone. It was wrong of me to assume you wouldn't care."

"Thank you. I accept your apology." She picked at her short fingernails the way she always did when nervous or when she had something on her mind. "Would you like to stay for supper? My way of saying thanks for giving Rory and me a lift."

Now that stunned him silent for a moment. She was actually asking for time with him? There had to be an ulterior motive.

And he wanted to know.

"Sure, if you don't mind." It would give him a chance to map out some thoughts he had for keeping Rory too busy to get into trouble. "It's a long way back into town and this day was a real kick in the pants. But on one condition."

"What's that?" She eyed him warily.

"You let me help. You've had a long day, too."

Smiling, she pushed to her feet. "I have a better idea. I'll have something delivered from the ranch's kitchen. We can sit out here and decompress. The mood gets rather heavy in the cabin with Rory's attitude."

"Teenagers can be mercurial." He stood facing her, close enough to touch. So close he could have smoothed back a blond lock.

"*Mercurial?* Perfect word," Charlotte answered, tugging off her hair band and repositioning it securely again. "What made your day a kick in the pants?"

He watched every move of her slim hands, remembering the silken texture of those golden strands. "One of my patrolmen was out with an appendicitis, so I spent the day filling in writing speeding tickets."

A smile teased at her pink lips. "Well, that's not the dangerous story I was expecting."

Her laugh twined around him, smoking inside

him in tempting tendrils. Against his better judgment, he wanted her. He felt the magnetic draw, as present as ever. His hand lifted, as if of its own volition—

Only to be stopped short when the door was yanked open, the space filled by Rory holding a soda can. “So, has she finally told you that she’s pregnant?”

Chapter Five

Charlotte couldn't remember when she'd been so angry with her brother. Hurt, too. How dare he so cavalierly announce her pregnancy? How dare he blow up her life that way? If he didn't get out of her sight immediately, she would say something she regretted.

Besides, she had to deal with Declan, who was currently standing frozen on her porch, his handsome face creased with shock. And she couldn't blame him. What an awful way to find out about surprise fatherhood. How she wished she'd already told him.

"Rory," Charlotte barked, pointing, "go back into the cabin. Now. We'll talk about this later."

Her brother opened his mouth—to argue, no doubt. But he'd pushed her too far this time.

"I mean it." She didn't raise her voice. She didn't have to. She pinned him with a look that she hoped relayed the depths of her fury, and pain over what felt like such an epic betrayal. "Not. One. More. Word. You're done."

The teen actually looked a little regretful, like he knew he'd crossed a line. He didn't argue as he turned back to the door, pausing just long enough to let Rosie scamper in ahead of him before closing the door behind them.

Silence descended, broken only by the gurgle of the brook in front of her place and the tinkle of paw print wind chimes hanging from her porch. Sounds that usually soothed her. Not now, though.

Slowly, she turned back to Declan, weighing her words, trying to figure out what she could say to ease the sting of him learning about the baby this way. She drew a blank. He deserved better. She'd made a mistake.

"I'm sorry you had to find out this way," she began, the weight of what she'd done lying heavy on her. "I intended to tell you soon."

His shoulders were braced. A pulse throbbed in his temple. "Is it true? What he said? You're pregnant?"

"Yes. And it's yours." Nerves fizzed through her veins, making her light-headed in a way that had nothing to do with pregnancy. She inhaled deeply, the fragrance of spring blooms flooding her senses. But there was a tightness in her chest that could not be undone even by the sanctuary she'd lovingly created on the front porch. All of these thriving plants around her radiated so much life. And everything with Declan felt frostbitten, in decline. "I didn't want to tell you over the phone. Then I didn't know you'd returned. The whole situation with Rory sidetracked things. I realize those are all excuses. I just want you to know that I didn't intend to keep this a secret for forever..." Pausing, she caught her breath. "Well, say something. Please."

He sagged back against the porch post, the sun setting behind him. The start of night sounds swelled from the forest—a hooting barn owl, croaking frogs, nocturnal wildlife coming awake. "I see now why you were upset with me for not calling when I got back."

Was it really going to be that easy? He didn't blame her? Instead, he was letting her off the hook?

Relief weakened her knees and she leaned against the post opposite of him, threading her fingers through the wind chime once, then letting her hand drop to her side. "It's sure a sign of how disconnected we are. Which is why I didn't tell you right away. I didn't want to make things worse between us."

"But now that I know, there's no more shutting me out." His jaw set with determination. "This is my baby, too, and I will not be shoved aside. We will figure out how to parent—together. I will not walk away from my responsibility."

She winced at the word *responsibility*. Yes, it was

the correct way to describe his tie to their child. Honorable even. But still, she'd half hoped for… What?

Something—anything—more.

Studying her with that narrowed cop-gaze, he said, "Being responsible is a good trait."

"Of course." Shifting her weight, she brushed against the bright white pot filled with a thriving mountain laurel, startling a bee into flight.

"Are you regretting the breakup?"

Now wasn't that a loaded question? More importantly to her, did *he* regret it? "We both had our reasons. Those haven't changed."

Such as—he wasn't a white-picket-fence guy. She was already overwhelmed with the personal relationships in her life. She didn't have the emotional bandwidth for more. And when she'd asked him for a break, he'd just walked away instead.

They'd never exchanged promises. No words of love had come from either of them.

"Something *has* changed, though, Charlotte." He looked down at her stomach. "We're expecting a baby."

She clenched her fists to keep from covering her expanding belly protectively. And perhaps to keep herself from reaching for him, throwing herself against his rock-solid chest and breathing in the familiar scent of him. She needed to keep things between them civil and as distant as possible to protect her from temptation. "I'm well aware. I'm glad you want to be a part of our child's life, but we have few months to hammer out those details."

Declan extended one booted foot and lightly teased at the toe of her high top. "It would be much simpler to discuss those details if we move in together."

Declan wasn't sure where those words had come from, but once out of his mouth, he wasn't calling them back. He was committed. To the proposition, of course. Smart or not, he wanted to move in with her, to make sure she was protected and cared for during the pregnancy.

And after?

Right now, *after* was a long way away. He cared most about this moment—which was not going well, judging by the horror on Charlotte's face. Ironic, since if anyone had the right to be angry, he did. He wasn't buying her story about planning to tell him soon. There was no evidence to back that up. She'd had plenty of time during their walks.

And what about when she'd fainted yesterday? He had every reason to fear she might exclude him if he didn't become a presence in her life. One she couldn't conveniently ignore again.

Charlotte's throat moved in a long swallow. "What did you just say?"

"We should move in together," he repeated.

"That's a little extreme, don't you think?" She fidgeted with the hem of her Top Dog T-shirt.

Right where his child rested.

How had he not noticed before?

The thought threatened to steal the air from his lungs. He'd never planned on being a father so he had no past dreams or intentions to call upon. He could only forge ahead and hope his instincts steered him in the right direction. "I can help you keep watch over Rory. You'll get more rest."

She eyed him warily as the porch light flickered on. "What do you get out of this?"

"I'll be a part of this baby's life." His kid. He pushed back thoughts of his own chaotic childhood.

Charlotte waved dismissively. "You can do that from your own home."

"I guess a proposal of marriage is out of the question, then." He'd meant the words as a joke. But instead of lightening the tension, he'd thrown fuel on the fire.

Her eyes went wide with shock. She even opened and closed her mouth twice before snapping back, "Totally out of the question. And I don't know why you would even bring that up. You don't mean it."

"Charlotte, take a breath. I was teasing." He remembered when they used to laugh together. Those days seemed very far off. "But I am serious about moving in together."

"And I'm serious in turning you down." She flipped her hair back over her shoulder, a steeliness turning her lush mouth that smiled so easily into a thin, determined line.

"Care to give me a reason?" Not that he'd really expected her to agree, but an answer might give him clues to what was knocking around in her head.

"For starters, I already have a home here." She counted off on her fingers. "That place is near my job. Rory just got settled in and doesn't need any more turmoil in his life."

"Then I'll move in with you," he said, not that he expected her to agree to that, either.

"I don't recall inviting you." She sighed, her gaze dropping to the potted plant in front of her. For a few moments, silence thundered in the space between them before she lifted her fingertips to her temple in a soft massage. Eyes fluttered closed, she continued, "Why are you even pressing this when you broke up with me? You've made it clear you're not interested in forever. Moving in together would just be an explosion waiting to happen, which would make it tougher to co-parent this baby. If that's what you really want."

"I do. I want that very much." More than he could have imagined for a pregnancy he hadn't even known about until tonight. Now wasn't the time to argue that even though he'd been the one to end things between them, he'd sensed her pulling away. She'd asked for a break, but he'd known they were over.

"Then you have to know kids need—and deserve—stability. We can't be some on-again, off-again couple."

"Fair point about stability." He knew that firsthand.

"I figured you would understand that from your experience on the police force."

"And from my own upbringing." He gestured to the porch swing in an unspoken invitation to sit on the planked space full of pillows with floral patterns. Once she settled, he joined her and toe-tapped the swing into motion. "Remember what I said at dinner with the O'Briens about the Guard duty striking a nerve?"

"You hinted that you had a troubled childhood." Her hair swished as the swing moved, the porch light and moonbeams playing off the blond strands.

"It was about more than that." He pushed aside one of the throw pillows, more for something to do than out of any uneasiness. Sharing didn't come naturally to him. "I was in and out of foster care."

"Oh, no. You never told me." She placed a hand lightly on his knee, empathy lighting her blue eyes. "I'm so sorry. That had to have been rough."

"I should have said something to you. It's not a secret..." But telling her would have brought more emotion into their relationship, an implied extra layer of trust, the start of building something more at a time when he'd already been struggling to keep himself from wanting more from their affair.

And wasn't that thought a cold dose of reality about why Charlotte had found it hard to tell him about the pregnancy? No doubt she shared all those same reservations times a thousand, given the import of the news.

"I'd like to know more, if you're comfortable sharing." Her soft voice called him back to an unhappy topic he'd rarely offered up to anyone.

"I wouldn't say I'm comfortable discussing it—ever. But we share a future now through this baby, so you have a right to know."

"I'm listening." She squeezed his knee once before removing her hand.

Her touch lingered, soothing and arousing all at once. He allowed himself the indulgence of stretching his arm out along the back of the swing. Her silky hair feathered along his skin. So often, they sat just this way, enjoying the moonlight and stars twinkling through the trees. So normal. So different from his world growing up.

"I never knew my father. He left right after I was born." Yet another reason he wasn't bailing on his progeny. On his responsibilities. "Mom worked hard. I know she loved me and wanted me in her life, but it was difficult going it alone. Mom would get it together, then things would fall apart again."

"How so?" she probed softly.

"It wasn't drugs or alcohol. A string of bad luck started a domino effect. She was fired from her waitressing job—the first time—so I went into foster care while she steadied her finances. She got me back, and then the car broke down. Back into foster care." Each one worse than the other since he became more difficult to place. "More lost jobs. All that change wore on me. I made bad choices. I landed in juvie."

"Juvie? I'm not sure I understand." Her forehead furrowed in confusion. "You're a police officer… the sheriff."

"Juvie records are sealed, so at eighteen I had a clean slate." Legally, anyway. The crimes still lingered in his memory, calling for him to atone every day when he put on his uniform. He gripped the smooth wood of the swing, anger at his past making him grip until the edge bit into his palms. "The whole experience was a wake-up call for me. I got my life together. I just want for Rory to figure things out before he goes that far, you know?"

"Me, too." She glanced back at the house, then returned her blue-eyed gaze to him.

"I care about the kid."

"I know you do." She picked up the lilac-embroidered pillow from between them and hugged it against her chest. "And I appreciate that you're willing to help him, even though we're broken up."

As if he needed reminding.

"I have even more reason now," Declan pointed out. "He's the uncle to my child." He cleared his throat as the baby became that much more real to him. He found himself picturing a little fella with Rory's blond shaggy hair. "I think we've both talked enough for one night. Just think about what I said, if not about moving in, then at least about my role in our child's life."

She nodded. "I will. I promise."

The vow wrapped around him and held. She'd always been honest with him, a fact that kicked him in his conscience for doubting her. If she said she'd intended to tell him about the baby, then he should have believed her. Times like these, the past really sank its claws even deeper into him, creating doubts.

Their eyes met and held, the silence between them different, the air charged. Because everything had changed in the space of a few minutes. There was no going back to his solo life.

And there was no going their separate ways.

Rory shoved his bedroom window up, swung one leg over and reached for a fat tree branch, knowing he had to make his getaway fast before his sister could get inside and set the security system. He figured he didn't have much longer to make his escape. His sister was probably just about done talking to Declan on the porch. He felt kinda guilty for selling out his sister that way about the pregnancy.

If she'd just gotten mad, it wouldn't have been as bad. But seeing the hurt in her eyes, too?

Still, what was done was done.

And the last thing he wanted to do was think about what Charlotte having a baby would mean for his life.

Bringing his other leg over, Rory held tight to the branch and hefted himself out. He'd snuck out often enough to hang out with his friends, but tonight was more important.

Tonight, he was meeting a girl—Olivia.

They'd been texting since they met in the barn. When she'd asked for him to meet her tonight for a walk, no way would he have turned her down.

Steadying himself on the tree limb, he carefully made his way down, branch by branch. He figured afterward, he would go back to the cabin and just sleep on the porch. When Charlotte turned off the alarm in the morning, he could fake like he'd gone out there while she was in the shower. He'd even changed clothes so she wouldn't get suspicious seeing him in what he was wearing before.

It was a solid plan with a chance of working.

His foot hit the thick carpeting of pine straw. He turned on his cell phone flashlight and made tracks toward the barn. The mountain air turned chilly at night, even in the spring. That gave him the perfect excuse to wear a hoodie, with less chance of someone recognizing him.

Luckily, there were enough guests milling about that he could blend in. He dodged around an older couple taking a walk. Waited for a hayride to amble past. Then set off jogging.

He darted along the path. The sound of his steady breathing mingled with the distant but familiar notes of Raise the Woof, Top Dog's country band, performing for the rodeo night. One of the horses in the pasture that connected with his path whinnied as he ran by. For a moment, the horse trotted next to him, keeping pace on the other side of the fence.

One look at Olivia standing under a lamppost

made all the effort worthwhile. She wore three-quarter-length leggings and a loose sweatshirt, her pretty hair all silky and draped forward over her shoulder. And when she smiled, he felt like the most important person in the world.

Not many people were happy to see him. Nobody really, except her, which made being near her all the more potent.

Extending her hand, she clasped his. "Thanks for meeting me here. You've been so busy, we've hardly had time to talk."

"Your hand is cold. I hope you weren't waiting too long." He clasped both of her hands in his, glad he had the excuse of warming her up to touch her. "Did your parents give you any trouble about leaving?"

Shrugging, she looked at the ground, scuffing her gym shoes through the dirt. Her plump lips tightened as she swallowed. "They don't even know I'm gone. They're too busy fighting. I had to get out of there."

"Is everything okay? Like how bad are they arguing?" His mom had had a boyfriend once who'd slapped her so hard she'd gotten a black eye. His mother had insisted it wouldn't happen again. He hadn't known what to do, so he'd told Charlotte.

His sister had chewed the guy out and threatened to call the cops if he didn't get out of their lives for good. She was fearless like that.

Another twinge of guilt shot through him as he thought of how he'd treated her lately. But it was like a jail around here these last few months.

Olivia turned her hand in his to link fingers with him. "Like getting-divorced bad. Dad seemed to think if we came here with some happily married friends that would make Mom magically forgive him for all the crummy stuff that's happened."

He wanted to ask what kind of crummy stuff, but that seemed too nosy. Instead, he settled for a simpler question.

"Why did your mom come, then?" He wished he could comfort her, but he didn't know her that well. He liked her and didn't want to spook her or disrespect her.

"She heard this place has magic and she hoped it would make him go away." Her voice dripped with sarcasm.

"Man, that sucks."

"At least some of my friends are here, too." She brushed off his sympathy with a smile and scrunched nose. "And I've made a new friend."

"Yes, you have." He squeezed her hand.

She smiled for a moment or two, just staring back at him before she nodded toward the barn. "How did you get a job here?"

"Um, it's not a job exactly." If she had questions about how to apply, he wouldn't have any answers to give her, but he couldn't tell her the truth about his work, either. The last thing he wanted was for her to know what a screwup he was. "I, uh, volunteer to help with the horses."

"That's really nice of you." She looked at him like he was some kind of hero.

Guilt stung—again. "My sister kinda pressured me. I, uh, spilled some paint in the gift shop and I need to make up for the stuff that got messed up."

"Well, whatever. I'm just glad I got to meet you," she said, all flirty and stuff batting her eyelashes. "It's making this vacation much more interesting."

"Glad I could be of Top Dog service." He gave her a wink that he hoped didn't look too lame. He knew he wasn't cool. But for some reason, Olivia was giving him attention.

Shoulder-bumping him, she clasped his hand tighter. "So, what else is there to see around this place? I figure we've got a couple of hours before anyone notices we're gone. Wanna give me a personal tour?"

And even knowing there would probably be consequences a lot worse than mucking out horse stalls if he got caught, Rory was all in.

Chapter Six

When Charlotte woke up the next morning, for the first time since she'd found out she was pregnant, she didn't feel sick.

Her morning went much faster when she didn't have to lie in bed eating crackers and sipping ginger ale. She finished her shower, tossed on a pair of khaki overalls and was ready to take Rosie out well ahead of schedule. A much-needed positive sign after yesterday's debacle with her brother spilling the beans to Declan about the baby. At least the news was finally out there, something to be thankful for in the midst of so much still left unsettled between them.

Taking a deep breath, she pushed aside the worries threatening to steal her morning's peace. Later, she'd deal with her concerns about what her next conversation with Declan would hold. She'd promised to call him tomorrow. But for now, she had time to gather her thoughts and shore up her defenses. She had at least thirty minutes all to herself to enjoy before her brother woke up and she intended to make the most of it.

Early morning sun streamed through the blinds as Rosie hobbled across the wood-planked floor, her nails clicking.

"You feeling okay, girl?" Charlotte knelt to massage the dog's back hips. Shortly after adopting Rosie, she'd taken the dog to the veterinarian for a checkup. The pup had needed a good teeth cleaning and two teeth pulled. And she had arthritis, but no more than normal given her age.

The level of relief at the clean bill of health had surprised her. Rosie had only been a part of her life for a couple of months, but the scrappy little senior pup had sure wagged her way into Charlotte's heart as if she'd always been there.

After another scratch, Rosie shook herself, once, twice, and then wobbled toward the door again. Charlotte pulled her cell phone from her pocket to disarm the security system, only to remember she'd already taken care of it before her shower. She snagged a Top Dog sweatshirt and pulled it over her head, the morning, mountain air usually crisp.

Opening the front door, she stepped aside for her dog, then followed Rosie down the steps. The veterinarian had warned her that owls and hawks could scoop up small animals in this part of the country, so she stayed on her guard when Rosie was outside.

She jammed her feet into her faded Crocs by the doormat before rushing down the steps into the yard. She moved so fast to keep up with Rosie she almost stumbled over…

Her brother?

Rory was kneeling in the flower bed, pulling weeds. Most days, he wasn't even awake at this hour, much less immersed in manual labor.

Blinking fast to clear her vision, she half thought she must be hallucinating. But nope. Her brother was backing out of the shrubs with a fistful of dandelions, taproots dangling between his fingers. The image called to mind memories of him in preschool, with a straggly bunch of wildflowers he'd picked for their mother.

A lump lodged in Charlotte's throat. "Careful there. The bees are crazy active right now. What has you up so early?"

"Just trying to make things right with you, for what I said last night. I know how important your garden is." Morning sun washed his movements in gold hues as he adjusted his grip on the plants.

The words soothed a raw spot inside her.

It wasn't a full-on apology, but it was a start. She appreciated that he recognized how hurtful his actions had been. "On a Saturday?"

"Yep. I just got started, though." He sank back

on his bottom in the grass, tugging the string on his hood.

That made sense. She'd only disarmed the security system about thirty minutes ago before her shower. Rosie sprinted into the yard, diving into the line of shrubs alongside the cabin.

"Well, thank you. I appreciate the effort." Apologies were hard. And perhaps she owed one to him as well for not telling him sooner. Walking to the tire swing hanging from a fat oak tree, she sat, studying her brother as she swayed. "Do you want to talk about what happened last night? About my being pregnant?"

"What's there to say?" He shrugged, his hoodie rippling on his thin frame.

"How did you figure it out?" she asked as Rosie rolled to her back, itching along her spine.

Rory plucked at the lawn absently, his jaw tight. "I saw a bill from the doctor on the table."

Hearing the dejection in his voice, she realized how upset he must have been, what a shock it would've been when his world had already been tossed in a blender lately. "I'm sorry you had to find out that way."

Her brother picked apart a weed, tearing blades, avoiding her gaze. Plant strands feathered downward, drifting in the light breeze. "Are you and Declan gonna move in together?"

"No. This doesn't change the fact that we broke

up. Obviously, he will be in our lives more now. He wants to be involved with the baby for the long haul."

He snorted on a dark laugh, tossing aside the shredded clump. "Like our dad did?"

"Declan is not even remotely like our father," she said quickly, sincerely. Charlotte leaned forward in the swing, her toe anchoring in the dewy grass. "This also doesn't change things with us. You're my brother. Your home is right here."

He rubbed his dirty hands together with exaggerated care. "What about when Mom gets out of the hospital?"

"That could be quite a while in the future." If ever. She scooped up Rosie and settled the pup on her lap, taking comfort in threading her fingers through the silky curls.

"Yeah, and she probably won't be able to handle me coming back right away."

"You could be right," she said. No need soft-soaping how ill their mother was. No need to get Rory's hopes up. "It sucks, and I hate for you that this is the way things are. But I want you to know you can count on me. Always. I'm here for you. You're family."

Scrubbing a sleeve under his nose, he nodded. "It wasn't all bad, though. With Mom, I mean."

"Of course not. She loves us." That had never been in doubt. Their mom had tried and the good times needed to be remembered, celebrated. "Remember when she took us on that surprise trip to the beach?"

He grinned, a chunk of blond hair falling over his forehead. "She packed a cooler full of peanut butter and jelly sandwiches, apples and lemonade."

"We forgot towels," she added, the memory picking up steam in her mind. "She had us dry off using the hand dryers in the public restrooms."

"People were staring." His smile faltered. "But I just kept thinking they were jealous that our mom was so innovative."

"And she was. She still is," Charlotte said, willing him to believe her. "She's trying her best. I know that deep in my heart. I hope you know it, too."

"Yeah, whatever." He eyed her sideways. "Do you worry this kid will have mom's disease?"

Shock snapped her back so forcefully Rosie leaped from her lap and Charlotte grabbed the swing's ropes to steady herself. "Um, I hadn't thought about it."

Rory shot to his feet, dusting himself off. "Forget I said anything. I'm gonna go shower."

Charlotte thought about following him, pushing the conversation further, especially on the subject of their mom. But she also worried about making him clam up again and retreat into his shell. She'd assumed he was depressed because of their mom.

Could he be depressed *like* their mom?

Even the thought made her eyes sting with tears for her baby brother. Maybe she should talk to their mom's counselor about help for him. If he would even go.

She rested her head against the swing's rope just

as Rosie bounded into the pile of discarded weeds, a sign of her brother's implied apology. Maybe that was the answer. For now, she would take heart in the fact that her brother was trying.

Because heaven knew, she had her hands full dealing with the mess she'd made of things with Declan and his impending fatherhood.

Declan had wrestled through the night with finding the perfect excuse to see Charlotte today. He wanted to nail down plans for his participation in his child's life. Starting with accompanying her to doctor visits.

Thank goodness the perfect excuse fell in his lap when Jacob had called him this morning, regarding a security concern.

So now, here Declan stood, in the middle of the pasture by the stables, surveying the clear signs of vandalism. In the middle of the night, someone had driven out into the pasture and done doughnuts, spinning out and tearing a wide and ugly swath through the grass. Declan hated to think it could have been Rory. He reminded himself of Charlotte's reassurance she would set her security system and that she'd changed the code, without giving Rory the number.

Taking photos of the tire treads with his cell phone, he half listened to Charlotte and Jacob talking through the damage while Hollie pulled security footage from the computer in the stable office.

Charlotte adjusted her hold on Rosie's pink rhinestone leash. "We're not going to be able to regrow this in time for the May Day festival."

Her weary voice carried on the breeze. As much as he wanted to look at Charlotte, to comfort her, he needed to focus on business, too.

Standing by his stallion, holding the reins, Jacob sighed, sweeping his Stetson from his head and scrubbing his wrist across his brow. "Throwing down sod would require closing the area off to horses. Given the placement, that would also create all sorts of problems with riders getting from the barns to the trails."

Already, the regular traffic flow of events seemed congested. Sightseeing groups on horseback were waiting for a hayride to amble away. Delays were unheard of at the ranch, where lines were considered bad business. A class for yoga with dogs—doga—had been shuffled closer to the campgrounds. The petting zoo had been relocated into the arena. Those temporary fixes would work for now, but eventually they would run out of options. Whoever had done this had done real damage to the ranch business. Declan zoomed in on a candy wrapper by one of the treads.

"Well," Charlotte said, walking past, her overalls rolled up to her knees showing her tiny floral anklet, "we could disguise the area. Put the covered wagon in the barest spot. I can spruce it up with flowers on the bench seat—out of reach of the horses, of course."

Jacob nodded, slapping his hat back on his head and patting his stallion on the neck. “We’d planned to do a sleepover option for a group of scouts in the wagon, but we can move them to the caboose cabin.”

“Okay, and for the rest of the area, we can build an extra wooden hay stand.” Her face lit with inspiration as bright as the late morning sun glinting off her golden hair. “Perhaps have the children paint messages and flowers on it.”

“Great idea,” Jacob said, fidgeting with the leather reins.

“It’s not the whole answer,” Charlotte said with a sigh, “but it’s a start.”

Jacob drew his stallion closer. “I’m going to check on what’s keeping Hollie.”

In a fluid movement, Jacob hoisted himself into the saddle. A clicking noise brought the horse to attention. Midday sun beat down, the shadows of Jacob and his horse practically nonexistent as they made their way toward the stable.

Leaving Declan alone with Charlotte.

He tucked away his cell phone, done taking photos for now. “Any thoughts on who did this?”

“Not Rory,” Charlotte said, relief coating her voice. “I had the security system set, with a new code, as planned. Could it have been Kai or Truitt?”

“I’ll be checking in with their parents.”

“I’m just glad it wasn’t my brother this time. I think the event at the gift shop has shaken him up. He actually weeded the garden this morning—without being asked."

"That's great news." Although he wasn't ready to trust the boy had changed so quickly. At least Charlotte had gotten some help for a change. "You need to take care of yourself. When is your next doctor's appointment? I want to be there."

Her mouth went tight and she scooped up her dog, rubbing Rosie's ears like a comforting talisman. Panting, the pup leaned into the touch, brown eyes full of appreciation that Declan understood perfectly. Charlotte always had a way of making everyone—humans, plants and animals alike—feel loved. "I'll give you a full report."

He wasn't going to be deterred that easily. "But shouldn't you be able to hear the heartbeat? I don't want to just be told about it. I want to be there."

"Understood," she said, her face softening a hint. Rosie licked her hand as if in reassurance. "Next visit, there will be more than the heartbeat. I'm having an ultrasound."

An ultrasound? Alarm zinged through him. "Is something wrong?"

"It's routine." She rested a hand on his arm, squeezing lightly.

"Will they be able to tell the gender yet?" Things were happening so fast. Well, for him anyway. She'd had time to get used to these milestones. "Not that I have a preference about the gender either way."

"Probably not. I think they said that will come

later in the pregnancy." She slid her hand away, stroking Rosie again, smoothing down the black-and-white fur.

He waited for her to continue, but when she didn't speak or move away, he said, "Does this mean I'm invited to the ultrasound?"

Again, she paused so long he thought she might argue, as she'd done about moving in together. Although he doubted she would cause a scene, not with so many guests milling about.

Finally, Charlotte gave him a simple nod. "I'll message you the date and time."

Relief made his heart hammer right beneath his badge. He may have lost the battle on moving in together—for now—but he was making progress. He would need to work hard to get back in her good graces.

Luckily, he was a man used to working hard for what he wanted in life. Because no way was he letting his child grow up with an absent father.

Doctor visits were sure different with Declan at her side. He hadn't been pushy during the appointment, but his presence loomed large since he'd picked her up to drive her there.

Now, they were each the proud recipients of an ultrasound photo of their healthy child.

The awe of the moment still wrapped around her as they walked out of the doctor's office, into the parking lot—awe and the unnerving realization that this was really happening. She and this handsome, charismatic man were going to have a child together.

Which made it all the more difficult to tamp down her attraction to Declan. More than anything, she wanted to lean against his chest, feel his strong arms wrap around her.

Well, more than *almost* anything.

Her top priority? She wanted—needed—to figure out a plan for how to juggle parenthood with a man who'd made it clear they were over.

Declan held the tinted door open, allowing her to step out from the warm lights of the doctor's office into the bright sunshine of the afternoon. Tucking a strand of hair behind her ear, she waited for Declan to step through the threshold before approaching a small, but relatively full parking lot at the end of Main Street, a narrow two-lane road down the middle of Moonlight Ridge, Tennessee. The quaint town had quickly become home to her, offering her the peace and sense of belonging she'd missed in her chaotic childhood.

His boots thudded softly as they walked down the sidewalk, cool wind stirring her hair. Quiet stitched the space between them, allowing for the hum of trucks and the conversations of birds to become their soundtrack. A narrow river—more of a stream really—rushed by in the distance. It was the same one that flowed to the cave and hot springs on the ranch. It formed the basis for the legend that started the whole O'Brien family legacy.

Something about how the Queen of the Forest led people to the cave where they found a lost puppy, hungry and dirty. As they rinsed the puppy, their bond was renewed. Healed. Like magic. They found a way to work with the land, with each other. And after that, people swore the animals tapped into the mystical, bringing healing to those in need.

An idea tugged at the edges of her imagination for ways to include that story in the floral display for the May Day event. Cascades of blue flowers flowing like water.

But she needed to pay tribute to Moonlight Ridge as well, a town so small its boundaries melded seamlessly into the dude ranch. So much so, she quickly spotted people from the Top Dog sphere on the nearby streets.

There was elementary librarian Susanna Levine in the school parking lot with her pet therapy dog, Atlas, and future stepson Benji in tow. There was the Top Dog groomer walking out of the local animal shelter after volunteering.

The clop of horse hooves added percussion to the melody from birds in the trees. Squirrels danced from limb to limb.

This was a beautiful place to bring up a child, the kind of fairy-tale locale she'd dreamed of growing up. Her gaze dropped to the ultrasound photo in her hand.

Declan stayed in step with her, no doubt adjusting his longer stride to match her shorter one. "Let me buy you lunch."

The offer caught her by surprise. Mostly because she really wanted to say yes, even though she had piles of work waiting for her. She stopped walking, tilting her head to assess him as a couple passed them with a spirited Chihuahua mix. She thumbed the edge of the ultrasound photograph, exhaling as the tiny pup yipped and yapped at one of the elm trees ahead of them. "Don't you have to get back to work?"

"I have another hour." Pulling out his phone, he glanced through the calendar app. "I know a great little diner right around the corner, next to my office, that serves the best pulled pork. They even have fried pickles."

Her mouth watered at the prospect of food and, yes, sharing the meal with this man. "Really, you don't have to do that."

"Hey, this is a big day." He waved the ultrasound in the air. "Don't you want to be able tell our child about today? It will show us as a united front."

He had a point. And she was starving. What would it hurt to put a hold on worries, just for an hour? "Lead the way. But be warned, I'm placing a big order."

"Of course." Declan slid an arm around her shoulder, tucking her to his side. "Nothing's too good for the mother of my child."

Her heart stuttered, and her senses melted at his touch. So familiar. So exciting. She looked up into his brown eyes and tried to scrounge for words to back things up just a few seconds, when they were planning lunch.

Before he'd touched her.

A cleared throat saved her from having to figure out what to say. She startled, then found Doc Barnett just behind her.

"Well, hello," Nolan said, his gaze dropping to Declan's arm around her shoulder. "I was just heading out of the office for lunch. Sure didn't expect to run into two of my favorite people. How's everyone doing? I was worried about you after that fainting spell."

Declan's arm fell away and he tucked the ultrasound photo into his back pocket, staying silent.

She appreciated how he was leaving it to her to choose what to share.

"Actually," Charlotte said, "I fainted because I'm pregnant. Declan and I are expecting a baby in the fall."

Nolan's eyes went wide. "Congratulations." He thrust his hand out to shake. "That's fantastic news."

Declan clasped his hand in the firm shake. "We just had an ultrasound."

"Pretty mind-blowing, isn't it?" The doctor grinned wide. "No matter how long I practice medicine, it's still the highlight."

Charlotte had been so worried about the pregnancy up to this point that there hadn't been much time for celebrating. It felt good to share the joy. "We don't know what gender the baby is, but all looks healthy. And there aren't twins."

Nolan angled to the side out of the way of a couple of tourists, then continued, "Do you mind if I share the good news with Eliza?"

"Of course," Charlotte said wryly. "It seems the cat's pretty much out of the bag anyway."

"Good, good," Nolan said. "I'm sure Eliza will want to celebrate. We can do a couples' get-together with you, us and the O'Briens."

Couples?

The word set her back a step and stole her ability to answer. The sting of it was, she knew the assumption was logical. Especially since the good doctor had seen Declan put his arm around her. Logical, though, wasn't the same as true.

But right now likely wasn't the time to correct him. Better to get her story straight with Declan. They needed to come up with a polite explanation going forward for their friends who would assume she and Declan were a couple again once they heard about the baby. Because no doubt this kind of situation would come up again and again.

And while she couldn't deny she was still attracted to the father of her child, she couldn't afford to indulge. She couldn't risk the chaos of an on-again, off-again relationship. It wouldn't be fair to her brother or to the baby.

Or to herself.

Chapter Seven

Declan was a man of his word these days. Having thrown away his good name once before, he didn't intend to backslide.

So when he'd vowed to keep an eye on Rory and support the boy's horse-stall penance, Declan intended to follow through. Too bad keeping his word involved shoveling manure on a Saturday morning.

As Declan picked his way on the well-manicured path toward the stables, he took in the hustle and bustle of the ranch in the early morning. A couple dressed in matching Top Dog flannels carried a green canoe above their heads. A group of teenage boys slung red fishing poles over their shoulders, veering off the path to the right to the well-stocked lake.

Sticks crunched beneath his feet as he entered

the barn. The already bright morning sun made the transition into the barn's interior cause him to pause while his eyes adjusted. As his vision became accustomed to the warmer overhead lighting, he was greeted by Cricket's whinny as he walked by. Rory, his sleeves rolled up, was in the threshold of the last stall.

Declan snagged a shovel from against the wall and closed the distance between himself and the teen. "Taking a break?"

Rory jolted, then stuffed his cell into his jeans pocket. "Just because I'm doing community service doesn't mean I can't take a personal moment every now and then."

"Of course. And I can see you've been working hard." He gestured to the boy's dirty jeans.

Rory picked up his shovel again, eying Declan suspiciously. "What are you doing here?"

"I thought you could use a hand," Declan said, gesturing to the wheelbarrow full of manure in the center of the stall.

"Are you helping Kai and Truitt, too? Or are you only checking up on me?" Rory jammed the pitchfork into the closest stall floor, scooped and sifted the manure from the strands of hay before dumping the waste in the wheelbarrow.

The kid seemed to be getting the hang of this.

"Not checking up on. Only helping." Declan remembered well the feeling of not being special, not mattering to anybody. "Just you today."

"Because you're trying to get in my sister's good graces." Rory's grip on the wooden handle was so hard, his knuckles were white. Bright eyes narrowing, Rory shook his head dismissively, blond hair tumbling over his forehead.

"I wouldn't use you that way." Declan shoveled side by side with Rory, sensing that if he made too much direct eye contact the boy would close off. "I hope you know me better than that."

"Then why are you spending your Saturday morning cleaning stalls?" Rory pitched the manure fork into the wheelbarrow before exiting the stall, shooting across to the other side. He nearly crashed into another stable hand in the process. Rory propped open the next stall door, careful to work around the red roan gelding that chomped on the morning hay.

"You've been making a real effort and that deserves recognition." An honest answer. A savvy kid like Rory would sense BS a mile away.

"Let me get this straight." Rory jammed the shovel into a pile of hay and leaned on the handle. "You're here because I'm good at moving manure around?" Huffing in disbelief, he went back to work, giving Declan his back. Sweat already formed along his hairline.

"Your sister told me you were picking weeds to help her out." He wasn't sure the boy's motives had been pure, but he deserved props for trying. Declan stepped into the stall, stroking the red roan's silky neck while the handle of the manure fork rested against his chest. "That shows real maturing on your part."

Rory's shoulder hitched up for a moment before he answered, "It was just a few dandelions. Nothing to make a big fuss about." They shoveled in silence, their rhythms syncing. "With the baby and all, are you and my sister a thing again?"

"We're figuring things out. I can promise once we do, you'll be kept in the loop." Declan kept the steady pace. Working in tandem eased some of the tension between them. "I will be an active part of the baby's life. So you'll be seeing more of me. You okay with that?"

"I guess it's cool. The kid needs his—or her—dad."

He and Rory had that in common—a lack of a father figure. The red roan nickered, tossing its head before sniffing Declan's pockets. It seemed this horse anticipated treats. "You'll be a big part of the baby's life, too."

"Another reason for me not to be a screwup." Rory tossed aside the shovel. "I get it. You can stop preaching."

"I'm not trying to lecture." Declan picked up the tool and set it against the stall door. "I'm speaking from experience. I've been where you were—frustrated, angry, lashing out at a world that was beating the crap out of me."

Rory glanced sideways at him, a thick chunk of sweaty blond hair partially obscuring his face.

"Yeah, right. What did you do? Forget your homework and land in detention?"

If he wanted the kid to trust him, he needed to offer a part of himself in return. Declan glanced over his shoulder to where a stable hand was currycombing one of the trail horses. "Fell in with the wrong crowd and ended up in the back seat of a stolen car."

"Just a joyride though, right?" Rory asked with a half grin.

"First of all, there's no such thing as 'just' a joyride." Declan wasn't letting himself or Rory off the hook with that excuse. "No matter how you look at it, that's theft. And second of all, that 'joyride' was being used as a getaway car by two teens stealing junk food from a convenience store. Stupid."

Rory's smile faded to shock. "What did you take?"

"Me, personally? Nothing. I was in the back seat of the car asleep. But there were still consequences." And man, was he scared when he woke up and realized what had happened, all because he hopped out of the window of his latest foster home to hang with his "cool" new friends.

A wry smile slid back up Rory's face, creasing dimples just like his sister's. He absently stroked the gelding's neck as he fed him an oat treat from his left pocket. "You got in trouble and you didn't even get a bag of Skittles."

A surprise chuckle burst free. "Pretty much sums it up."

"Well, just because I'm mucking out stalls—"

Rory grabbed his shovel again "—don't expect me to join the police force someday."

"Deal," Declan said, picking up the rhythm again. Even if they didn't speak for the rest of the morning, they'd made progress. He could just hope that it would be enough to keep Rory on the right path. The teen was struggling. And if he kept getting into trouble, then it was just a matter of time before he went too far. Declan hated the thought of what that would do to Charlotte.

And look at that, his thoughts had circled back to Charlotte…as usual. So while he continued to work beside Rory, he allowed his mind to wander back to a time when his romance with Charlotte had been new…

Declan cradled his plate, making his way down the ranch's supper buffet, the echoes of bingo calls from across the entry mixing with the clank of silverware in the lodge's main dining area.

The food at the ranch was always top-notch, but he was starting to wonder if he would ever be able to talk Charlotte into a real date downtown. Even though he enjoyed the vacation vibe here, he couldn't forget that for Charlotte, sticking around here was like never leaving work. Even now, she'd left her place at the table to answer questions for a couple celebrating their fiftieth anniversary.

Exhaling hard, Declan scooped sautéed Vidalia onions and peppers over his grilled flat iron steak.

Garlic red potatoes and green beans. Biscuits and cobbler rounded out the meal.

It was all delicious... But how could he enjoy it when their meal kept getting interrupted by other people? He just wanted an uneventful evening to chill with his girlfriend.

Joining Charlotte back at their table in a corner purposely chosen for its distance from foot traffic to the buffet, he set down his dishes and pulled her chair out, motioning for her to sit. "M'lady."

"Thank you, Sheriff." She batted her eyelashes at him playfully as she slid into her seat. "Sorry it took me so long to join you."

"No need to apologize. You're well worth the wait." He drank in the sight of her in a flowing brown suede dress and boots, having clearly taken the time to change clothes for their dinner together. "I'm just glad you're here now."

Sighing, she draped her napkin over her lap, then sat up straight again, her eyes scanning while concern tightened her normally plump pink lips into a thin line. "Where's Rory?"

"Right over there." Declan pointed toward the dessert table, where the teen was flirting with a high school girl who worked part-time in the gift shop. A rare sighting of Rory without his eyes glued to his phone.

Charlotte smiled apologetically. "I feel like I need to put a tracker on my brother."

"That can be arranged," he said with a wink. Half

joking. He had a bad feeling about the kid and worried for him. And for Charlotte.

"No matter what I do, he works his way around it." Shaking her head, a strand of blond hair slid forward over her shoulder. "I have him turn on the locator on his cell phone and he just leaves his phone in the place he's supposed to be...then has a burner phone to call his friends when he leaves."

"How did you figure that out?" He reached for the plate of lemon wedges to add to his iced tea as a fiddle player wove around the tables.

"I was doing his laundry and a burner fell out. I opened it and saw the texting history. I hate being the kind of person who searches a kid's room, but I have to keep him safe."

Charlotte had been thrust into guardianship, and she managed to do all of this for her brother with a smile. She dazzled guests, too. But she seldom got a break, another reason Declan worried for her.

"There were more phones in his room?" He hated the alarms going off in his mind, but he recalled well the lengths he'd gone to as a teen to slip away.

Not to mention all the trouble he'd landed into. He didn't want to assume the worst about Rory, but he also didn't want to miss the signs.

Declan jammed a pitchfork into a pile of hay, feeling some of his earlier optimism slip away with the reminder that memory had brought. Because here they were again. Same problems. Same worries to plow through, because to shuffle aside those responsibilities for the sake of exploring his attraction to Charlotte would be selfish.

Going forward, he needed to focus on those who couldn't look after themselves—the baby, Rory and, yes, even Charlotte's mother, whom he'd heard about but never met.

He'd worked too hard to turn his life around from the troubled teenage years, to find an honorable path. He couldn't afford to lose sight of that when they went on the couples date this evening.

On the other hand… As much as he tried to tell himself otherwise, he couldn't deny that he was looking forward to having her all to himself.

Thank goodness morning sickness was a thing of the past, because Charlotte had needed every waking hour today to finish up her workload in time for the couples' dinner this evening. Luckily, Rory was signed up for movie night for teens at the ranch, which made planning easier. She was surprised he'd been so amenable to the idea. Usually, he complained about attending anything to do with ranch's packtivities.

At least she had help as she made wreaths of dried flowers for children to wear during the festival. Gwen had joined her since her triplets were practicing for the May Day play and Charlotte's worktable set up outside the greenhouse gave them both a bird's-eye view of rehearsal. Children of ranch staff gathered on a planked stage set up by a wagon.

Charlotte fluffed her blond hair, a breeze caressing her neck. Despite the circulating air, the unseasonably warm spring day had Charlotte thankful to be under a great big canopy with Gwen. The two women laid out all of their supplies until the table was piled high with ribbons, wire and bins of dried flowers.

"Careful, there's a bee," Charlotte warned, swatting at the insect over a bin of lavender. "They're busy this time of year."

"Whew, thanks," Gwen said, flipping her red braid over her shoulder as the twangy notes of a banjo began to sound in the distance.

Charlotte's gaze skipped toward the stable where she'd seen Declan enter, presumably to help Rory. What were they saying? Doing? She itched to go look in on them, but that probably wouldn't be wise—even if she didn't have dozens of floral headpieces to make. "Did all turn out well with the painting in the shop?"

"Looks good as new." Gwen unspooled the lavender ribbon with care, making sure to cut it the same size as the pale pink ribbons on the table. "Declan has Kai moving boxes of inventory to finish out his community service. I won't lie—I appreciate the help. I'm swamped."

The woman didn't look overwhelmed. With her

smooth braid and breezy cotton sundress, she could have passed for a tourist enjoying a relaxing day.

Charlotte looked out from the canopy tent to the assemblage of children rehearsing with the banjo player. Even from here, she could see their bright smiles. Her hand drifted to her stomach. "If it's any consolation, everyone around this place is in awe of you. How in the world do you juggle a full-time job and triplets?"

"Top Dog's perks for staff—free room and board," Gwen said, counting on her fingers, "along with use of the ranch's dining hall and childcare. A winning combination, as you'll soon learn, too."

"Thank goodness. I can't imagine how I would manage if I didn't have this place, these people. You're all like family." She paused, a twinge of guilt stinging harsher than any bee. She swallowed as banjo chords drifted on the wind, a lump forming in her throat as she thought about all the layers of complication in her blood family. "Don't get me wrong. I love my mom and my brother, but I can't lean on them."

"I get the impression you can lean on Declan." Gwen held up a wreath to adjust the bow, eying Charlotte through the middle. "He seems like a real stand-up guy."

"He wants to be a part of our child's life." Charlotte looked away, over to the stables again as if drawn by a magnet. With the banjo and the distant singing of the children, she felt a strange sense wash over her, flush her cheeks. "I'm thankful for that, truly, but..."

Gwen set the wreath onto the pile and turned her full attention onto Charlotte. "You just want some emotional support for yourself. Someone to share the struggles and joys."

Of course Gwen understood—and more. She was living through the same thing as a widow. More guilt heaped inside Charlotte as she wove the delicate stem of the flower into the wreath. "I didn't mean to sound selfish. I do realize how lucky I am that my baby has a father who wants to be a part of his or her life."

"Well, if we're being transparent here," Gwen said darkly, slumping back in her chair, "my husband had already checked out on us before he died in a car wreck. He had another woman—his mistress—in the vehicle with him."

Charlotte gasped, pressing a hand to her chest. "I'm so very sorry."

"I thought he was on a business trip." Gwen shrugged, returning to sift through a bin of flowers as if welcoming the distraction. "Turns out he'd taken her on our dream vacation."

Charlotte rested a hand on Gwen's and squeezed, wishing she could do more, but also knowing that sometimes being present was the greatest gift.

And wasn't that what Declan was trying to do? Be present? Like how he was helping Rory today. How he'd accompanied her on the doctor visit. Those were all honorable behaviors from an inherently honest man. She felt confident he wasn't trying to manipulate her or buy his way into her good graces.

Maybe instead of focusing on what they didn't have together, she should set her sights on enjoying what they had, one moment at a time, rather than looking ahead to roadblocks.

Starting with diving all in on their date night with friends.

As he held open the passenger door for Charlotte, Declan realized that he hadn't been this nervous on a date since he'd taken Jenny Smith to the senior prom. He'd been flat broke, in a friend's borrowed car and his foster father's suit, which had been a size too large.

The date had been a disaster, with a flat tire and ketchup spilled on his suit.

Hopefully, tonight would turn out significantly better. Not that he was looking for romance. He was still firm in his resolve to keep things level, steady, for the sake of Rory and the baby.

Easier said than done with Charlotte looking so lovely, her blond hair flowing down her back, her legs appearing all the longer in jeans and three-inch heels. Her matching black blouse breezed over her curves, making his hands itch to tunnel under the loose fabric.

The outing felt so...normal. Like a regular date for an established couple.

Dragging in a ragged breath, he followed her to the SUV, his heart thudding harder as he watched the easy glide of her stride, the subtle sway of her hips. And soon he would be alone with her in the vehicle.

Not for long, though. The ride would be short, since Doc Barnett lived halfway between the ranch and town. The evening would give him and Charlotte an opportunity to explain to their friends about the baby. And more importantly, put a lid on any assumptions that they were a couple.

The last thing he needed was having them spook Charlotte when things were already shaky enough between them.

After clicking to unlock the SUV, he helped Charlotte into the seat. Even the brief contact of their hands sent his mind and body on high alert. The sooner he got to the Barnett house, the better.

The SUV roared to life, and he steered down the gravel driveway. Deep orange and pink colored the sunset, washing the ranch in vibrant tones as he drove past the paw print signs and a cluster of guests on horseback.

Stealing a glance at Charlotte, he noted the way her neck craned as she looked out to the cabins and woods of the ranch. Making mental notes for work? He respected her attention to detail that gave life to such beauty at the ranch.

Returning his focus to the road, he guided the SUV toward the wooden covered bridge. With every minute that passed, he became more and more aware of Charlotte's intense gaze.

He glanced across at her, the hazy late day glow casting a halo around her. He cleared his throat. "So,

Rory's really okay with going to the ranch's movie night?"

"Seems so. And I don't have to worry since everyone who leaves the arena has to sign out. He has plenty of Top Dog employee eyes on him." She twirled a lock of hair around her finger, the golden rays of the setting sun making her look like a lithe fairy. "Thanks for spending time with Rory today. It's one thing to hang out with him. It's another thing entirely to help muck out stables."

Safe enough territory for discussion. Turning on the blinker, he looked at her. "I figured he deserved some reinforcement for picking those weeds."

"That was a surprise for sure." She adjusted the vents, the blast of air lifting her hair. "What did you two talk about?"

"This and that. Nothing big." He didn't want to discuss his own misspent youth right now. Jaw tensing even as he looked at the dip of the hill—a sight that normally afforded him some comfort. "How was your day?"

"Crazy busy preparing for the May Day festival. Gwen helped me make dozens of hair wreaths with dried flowers." She smoothed her hands along her jeans. "I'm thankful for her help. It's been a challenge catching up after repairing the damage done by joyriders."

"Joyriders?" he repeated, the word hitching in his brain after his discussion with Rory. Had the teen told his sister? Was that why she kept staring at him so intently? "What makes you think they were in a stolen car?"

"I guess I just meant the word in a prankster kind of way..." She shrugged, shifting in the seat, which brought her knee closer to him. The vents swirled her scent in the scant space. "Regardless, it's making for extra work at a time the staff is already stretched thin getting ready for the May Day celebration."

The SUV rounded the mountain bend with ease, and he couldn't help but think how thankful he was to be back here. Back with her. Even with all the complications.

He appreciated how easy she was making conversation. How ready she'd been to accept the invitation tonight. Both boded well for building on a fresh start between them—one where they would be able to raise a child together. If only this attraction didn't thrum through his veins every time he looked at her, reminding him that he couldn't muck up the new relationship with all the desires of the old one.

"I can pitch in," he said, struggling to keep his voice steady when his libido was pounding overtime.

"I wasn't hinting. I promise." She rested a hand on his arm as they idled at a stop sign. "More just venting. But thank you so much for offering."

Smiling, she leaned across the center console and kissed him.

Chapter Eight

Charlotte could think of a dozen reasons why she should have stayed in her seat, waited for him to leave the stop sign behind. But all her good intentions might as well have flown out that window.

After only ten minutes alone in the vehicle with Declan, hearing his genuine concern for her and her family had her tossing away reservations faster than she could say *lip-lock*. In a month where she'd felt like she had the whole world on her shoulders, his efforts to take on some of those burdens called to her on the deepest level.

Sinking into his familiar embrace was so easy, so natural. His palms caressing her back. Her fingers clenching in the heated cotton of his shirt.

The warm glide of his tongue over hers stirred

her memories of a time when they'd shared more. Everything. Or so she'd thought, only to have their relationship go up in flames.

That thought was enough to cool her passion now. It had hurt so much the first time he'd retreated. How would it feel for her now, when there was so much more at stake than her heart?

Pressing a hand to his chest, she eased back, resting her forehead against his. Their ragged breaths twined in the air between them. She'd been fooling herself, imagining that she could enjoy this date night while still keeping the physical attraction at bay.

Before she could find words again, he eased past the stop sign and accelerated the SUV, but only for long enough to pull off onto the shoulder. The mountainside blocking her view out the passenger side window. A sharp bend in the road giving them an edge-of-the-earth vibe as the panorama of a green fjord spilled out below.

For now, there was just the two of them and the sun sinking into the trees.

He threw the vehicle in Park and shifted in his seat to face her, leather creaking. "I thought we were focusing on the baby and your brother."

"I'm sorry for the mixed signals," she said, sagging back, searching for the best way to explain. Well, when in doubt, the best answer was honesty. "You're not wrong. That was my intent. But some selfish part of me wanted to pretend—for just tonight—that we're like any other couple heading out for an evening with friends."

His gaze dropped to her lips, a tic twitching the corner of one eye. "How far were you planning to carry that impulse?"

"I only intended to enjoy tonight." Saying it now seemed so reckless, like a plan that would turn out exactly as it had—with her in his arms. As she dipped her chin, her blond hair fell in front of her eyes, and she hoped the last rays of the descending sun would hide the flush of heat she felt crawling up her face. "And then my heart was tugged by your care with Rory and I was kissing you."

He cupped her face. "For what it's worth, I've been wanting to do that very same thing since I showed up on your doorstep."

Her eyes welled with tears and she swiped her wrist across her face. "Don't worry about me. It's just the hormones."

"Which thing are you blaming on hormones? The tears or the kiss?" he asked with a half grin.

"Both?" she answered with a watery chuckle, her gaze fuzzy and unfocused from unshed tears. Looking beyond him, she grounded herself, taking note of the trickling waterfall on the mountain. Deep inhale on a four count. A pause. An exhale for another count of four. Anything to keep her steady as the world seemed to sway and threaten her still-tender heart.

"I realize this is complicated, with the baby." He tucked a strand of her hair behind her ear.

"It's not just because of the pregnancy." She let herself savor his touch for a brief instant before easing back, newly wary of playing with fire. Closing her eyes to shut out his concerned face and the dying sunlight, she made herself repeat another round of deep breathing. "This is all so convoluted because we broke up. I can't fall back into a relationship with you just because I'm expecting. That's not fair to either one of us."

"And yet, you just kissed me."

True enough. More embarrassment warmed her face, and she looked away from him. She stared intensely at the budding green leaves of the nearby tree as she spoke. "Can we just call it a momentary weakness and move on with our evening?"

He studied her with those insightful cop eyes for a handful of heartbeats before extending his hand. "Truce. For tonight."

Clasping his hand in hers, she shook back, all the while too aware of the calluses on his fingers. Of how very much she wanted him. "And I promise not to kiss you again."

As he put the SUV back into Drive, he shot a look her way that spoke loud and clear. Odds were very high they would be battling the attraction many more times in their future. It had been easier to pretend all feelings between them had passed when they were far apart.

But now? Looking at a future all tangled up together?

They would need a hefty Top Dog miracle to sort this out.

Rory wondered if Olivia would let him kiss her.

He had reason to hope.

Once the lights went down for the movie, he'd scooted closer to her. When she hadn't moved away from him, he'd held her hand. His heartbeat had pounded so loudly in his ears, he could barely hear the video.

He had to confess, this event wasn't as lame as he'd expected. He'd only signed up so he could be near Olivia, so his expectations had been low for the actual gathering.

The flick was pretty good—a film about teenagers going to a soccer camp being held at a farm. A place kinda like the ranch. There was a sequel, which they would watch after taking a break for supper.

As the film cast flickering lights through the dim arena, he squeezed Olivia's hand and thought about stretching his arm along her shoulders. But he didn't want her to laugh at him. Being a guy was tough, figuring out when a girl was interested and when she was just being polite.

He looked around the small arena to see what other guys were doing. The space had a screen set up in one corner, and rather than uncomfortable stadium seating, they'd scattered beanbag chairs and futon sofas. Across the way, staff was quietly setting up tables with food. The arena was used for lots of things at the ranch—from rodeos to welcome events. Even parties.

There was this girl at school—Ember, the class president—who wanted him to ask the O'Briens if they would allow the school prom to be held here. He knew that Ember was only being nice to him because she wanted something. Why else would she make time for such a big loser?

At least Olivia liked him for *him*.

Probably because she hadn't seen him at school.

The movie credits rolled and the lights went back on. Olivia turned to smile at him, still holding his hand. "Do you wanna get some snacks? The food here's pretty good actually. I was expecting something like stale popcorn and watery lemonade, but there's pizza, little burger sliders, fries with cheese dip. And as much soda as we want."

She looked so pretty in her jeans and flowery shirt, his mouth dried right up.

Clearing his throat, he swallowed, praying his voice wouldn't crack. "It's one of the good things about living here. I get to eat however much I want from the kitchen. Mrs. O'Brien makes the best cookies and cupcakes."

"I'm just glad you got to come." Easing her hand free, she stood and dusted the wrinkles off her faded wash jeans. "It's been tense in our cabin—too many families in there together. I like Zoey and Corrine, but it's getting old sleeping on bunk beds in the corner of our cabin's living area. But coming together was the only way my parents could afford this trip."

Walking alongside her toward the refreshments table, he watched the glide of her silky black hair. "How are you parents getting along lately? The ranch really helps people."

"They both stay so busy signing up for things the other one won't be attending, they don't have an opportunity to argue." She hooked arms with him and gave him a gentle shoulder bump. "But hey, at least that leaves me with more time to come by the stables to see you."

"It makes my day better for sure." That was a massive understatement. Glimpses of her were the bright spots that made the stable work bearable. But for how much longer? "When, uh, do you leave? Your spring break is probably just about over, right?"

"My friends and I are homeschooled online. Sucks that I have to do assignments during my vacation, but it is what it is. Anyhow, we're staying until the May Day parties. Then back to Ohio."

Ohio? Why hadn't he picked up on that before? "That's mighty far away."

"We can text," she reminded him as they took their place at the end of the line. "And maybe I can get a summer job here, doing something like what you do."

Now that was a big heaping dose of reality.

What if she found out why he was really working? She seemed like a nice person. He wished he'd met her before he'd gone along on that stupid prank with Truitt and Kai. Although if he hadn't been stuck shoveling out the stables, he might not have ever met her. He would be miserable sitting in his room playing video games with a bunch of strangers.

Before he could come up with something to say, Olivia's two friends joined them.

Zoey tugged at a perfect red spiral. "Well, hello, Rory. I'm surprised your jailer sister let you out for the evening."

Jailer? The word hit a little too close to home, given his recent brush with the law. "Charlotte just likes to know where I am."

And the more he thought about it, the more he figured it was better than if she didn't care at all. Zoey pursed her lips, eyebrows pinching together in what felt like heaps of unearned judgment. Was this what all girl groups were like?

Corrine tugged at the hem of her oversize band T-shirt—it showed the album cover of some rock group from a few decades back. "Do you live with your sister all the time?"

"Uh-huh. She works here." He rocked back on his heels, wanting to be done with this conversation.

Corrine narrowed her green eyes, arms crossing. "What happened to your mom and dad? Did they kick you out?"

Olivia touched her friend's arm, her cheeks a little pink. "Don't be such a brat. That's his personal business."

"Nah, it's okay." Rory jammed his hands in his pockets. He guessed it was normal for girls to grill their friend's potential guy. Not that he had much experience being the "potential guy."

"My dad's gone and my mother is so sick she's in a hospital… She's, uh, got tuberculosis."

Not a bad cover story.

He'd read about it in science class. It was better than sharing the truth. Charlotte kept saying their mom would get better someday, but he wasn't so sure. She'd been texting a lot lately and some of the messages sounded pretty out there. Super excited sometimes, with all these big plans for expensive vacations. She'd even promised a car once.

Then other times she was all depressed, apologizing for things in a way that made him uncomfortable. He didn't know what to say. He thought about asking Charlotte for advice, except he knew he didn't want to hurt his sister since their mom didn't reach out to her all that often. He worried she would make their mom stop messaging him altogether.

And the thought of not having his mother text at all felt even worse.

Corrine nodded, her short blond hair on the left side of her head rippling with the movement.

Zoey leaned in to whisper, her long silver earring swinging with the motion, "Do you think you can sneak out tonight? We're going swimming in the pond."

The thought of seeing Olivia in her swimsuit threatened to knock him right off his feet. And if she wore less than a swimsuit… He gulped.

Not that it mattered either way. He couldn't go. "My sister has been all crazy with the security system. I'm not sure I have the right code."

Corrine shook her head. "That's seriously messed up. Why doesn't she trust you?"

The words dripped with sweetness, but Rory didn't like the smile on her face. It was too wide and reminded him of the time he ate sour candies until his stomach ached.

Olivia put her hands on her hips. "Didn't you just ask him to sneak out?"

Rory appreciated her speaking up for him, but he had the sinking feeling this conversation was taking a downward spiral and he didn't know how to stop it.

Zoey twined the lock of hair tighter around her finger. "I heard Rory's just working in the stables because he got into trouble for breaking into the gift shop. That's probably why his sister won't let him do anything unless he's being watched like a kid."

Embarrassment stung. He saw the shock on Olivia's face, soon replaced by dawning horror. He'd known somebody like her wouldn't want to be with someone like him if she had the whole story—and now she did.

Pivoting hard, he ditched the food line and ran

straight for the door, past the checkout desk, chased by the sound of Olivia calling out his name.

With that kiss from Charlotte still firing through his veins, Declan struggled to pay attention to what was said during the couples' cookout. Doc Barnett had bought an old farmhouse, a sprawling property bigger than anywhere Declan had ever lived. The place appeared darn near perfect, but still Nolan talked about the renovations, happening in stages so they didn't have to wait to move in. He wanted his two grandchildren—Gus and Mavis—to have as little change as possible.

And he also wanted the place to be perfect for Eliza when they married.

To Declan's eye, the whole spread shouted white-picket-fence bliss for kids and adults. Trees to climb. Lounge chairs and a picnic table for adults, with a miniature version for children. And playground equipment—a massive wooden set with a fort and swings shaped like horses.

Doc had grilled kabobs and fresh corn at a stone outdoor cooking station, complete with a grill, smoker and additional burners. He had an arm looped around his fiancée as she scooped ice cream cones for the children. The air was filled with the squeals of kids mixed with the low hum of an outdoor speaker playing soft rock.

They'd been joined by the O'Briens, as well as Micah Fuller, a contractor for the ranch who was currently working on restoring the Barnetts' farmhouse. Micah had fallen for Susanna, the elementary school librarian, when attending a parent-teacher conference for his nephew who struggled with a learning disability. Susanna was there at his side while his nephew played with the other children.

Once the kids were settled with their dessert, the couples shifted to the side yard to play cornhole, women against the men.

Charlotte arced her arm back, then flung the small red bean sack toward the circular hole in the wooden board. The red beanbag slid on the smooth board, hovering on the lip of the opening. "Sorry again that we arrived late. We, uh, seemed to have caught all the red lights."

Susanna adjusted the clip in her hair as she chuckled, the jeweled piece shaped like a line of books. "There are only two between here and the ranch. I know since I drive the route from school to the ranch quite often."

"What can I say?" Charlotte shrugged. "Declan drives like a little old man."

Declan spluttered as the men laughed and jeered good-naturedly, clapping him on the back. He cleared his throat, then interjected, "Well, I *am* a police officer. I can't be setting a bad example to the public."

Susanna waved aside the notion. "No chance of that. You're a hero in this town, sheriff and military man. I was hoping you would come talk to the school kids during career week."

Hero? If only they knew life wasn't that simple. But that probably wasn't what anyone wanted to hear during a kids' circle time. "I'll check my calendar." He tossed his blue beanbag. And missed.

As Hollie took her turn, Charlotte stepped back and pulled out her cell phone. "I'm just checking in with Rory."

Hollie juggled a red beanbag from one hand to the other, a light breeze stirring the loose dark brown strands of her ponytail. "You're both doing a good job with him."

"Really?" Declan tipped his head to the side. "You can say that after the stunt he pulled at the gift shop?"

He hoped he was making a connection with the boy, but they had a long way to go to solidify a bond. He needed to be in a better position with the teen by the time the baby arrived, otherwise it would be too easy for the teen to slip through the cracks when their time and focus was taken up with the newborn.

"Childhood can be complicated," Hollie said, her eyes sharpening as she focused her attention on the wooden cornhole board. She bit her lip, exhaled loudly and sent the red bag soaring. It sank effortlessly in the hole, eliciting a whoop of joy from Eliza. "I'm not excusing his actions, but he's had a tougher road than many."

Susanna gathered up the tossed bags lying beside the board, moving out of the way so Micah could step forward for his turn. He overshot the hole by a smidge, the blue beanbag resting on the upper part of the circle. "Adjusting to a new family structure can be difficult—as most of us here can attest."

Declan scanned the yard, alive with children ranging from two years old to elementary school. Hollie and Jacob's four children had been adopted after their kids' birth parents died. Micah's nephew had come into his care because of the boy's mother's drug habit. And Doc Barnett was caring for his two grandchildren. The Top Dog Dude Ranch had a way of healing wounded hearts.

As this gathered group proved.

Susanna handed over the red beanbags to each of the assembled women. Her megawatt smile was warm. "Congratulations on the upcoming addition."

"Such great news," Hollie said before anyone could answer, then looked between Declan and Charlotte curiously. "Do you know if you're having a boy or a girl?"

Eliza pulled her blond hair back into a messy bun, concern feathering fine lines on her pale brow. "How are you feeling?"

"Well," Charlotte said, cradling her phone, returning to the game. "To answer each of you. Thanks. We don't know. And I'm feeling much better. But do you mind if I get a refill on the lemonade?"

Waving, Eliza motioned for the women to follow her to the elaborate spread of lemonade, sweet tea and fruit-infused water on the patio deck.

Once the ladies had moved out of earshot, Jacob adjusted the brim of his Stetson as Micah and Nolan moved toward their young children. Squeals of laughter rang out as they joined the kids' game of fairies and dinosaurs. Declan scanned beyond the immediate scene out of habit. Always assessing for threats, even in calm places and moments.

"So, Declan." Jacob stepped closer. "Any luck tracking down the vandals who tore up the grazing pasture?"

"No tips," Declan said, "and the security footage hasn't given us much to go on."

"It's like the person or persons responsible knew just where to go to avoid a full-face camera shot." Jacob scratched the back of his neck. "And that has me worried."

Astute observation. "Yeah, it appears it's someone who had access to the security cameras."

"I'll make sure the list is up to date," Jacob said. "But it's difficult to know for sure. Someone could have seen the monitors when coming to the office for a meeting…or even for a simple question."

Solving a mystery rarely came easily. "Have there been any other suspicious events? Anything at all?"

"Nothing I can recall, not since we caught bears tearing up a construction site a while back." He nodded toward Micah. "The staff still talks about him scaring them off."

"This definitely wasn't caused by a curious bear." Declan hooked his thumbs in his front pockets. He hated the niggling sense that this was somehow tied to Rory.

As Charlotte walked back with a fresh glass of lemonade, her cell phone alarm sounded, piercing the air and startling even the children. Declan straightened, his senses on alert. He recognized the sound of Charlotte's home alarm, piped through to her phone. He charged over to her, reaching for his work phone to alert the dispatcher.

Charlotte fished into her bag, digging around until her hand whipped out with her cell, clicking through to log in.

Palming her back, Declan asked, "Is everything alright? I'll have a car over there right away."

"Hold on." Charlotte raised a hand and showed him the camera view on her screen. "It's just Rory. He must have left the party without telling anyone."

Declan palmed the small of her back. "At least he went home. And he's alone, right?"

Nodding, she deactivated the alarm and tapped the speaker feature. "Rory? Are you okay?"

He stared into the security camera with angry eyes as he stood in the open doorway. "You don't have to check up on me every second, you know. The movie was boring and I figured I would let Rosie out."

As if on cue, the scrappy dog trotted out, shook herself off and scampered down the front steps. Rosie arched her back in a long stretch before trotting past the birdbath, to the flower bed, her nose to the ground. The bell on her rhinestone collar tinkled with each step.

Her forehead creasing with concern, Charlotte paced. "I'll be home in twenty minutes. We can spend some time together—light the firepit and have s'mores?"

As much as Declan regretted seeing an end to their evening, he knew this was the right call to make. And he intended to support her in her relationship with her brother.

Declan ignored the little voice inside that insisted he was just looking for any excuse to spend more time with Charlotte. Maybe even luck into another kiss. Or more. Even knowing how much it would complicate things didn't stop him from wanting to taste her again.

Reining in his thoughts, he focused on Rory's response.

"Sure, whatever." Frowning, the teen knelt by Rosie. The furball was pawing at her nose and rolling on the ground. "What do you have there, girl? Huh?"

Then he leaped back with a yelp, batting the air. "Bees! She's kicked up a nest of bees and they're everywhere!"

Chapter Nine

Charlotte's heart was in her throat as she sat in the passenger side of Declan's SUV, racing back to the cabin. Trees were a blur outside the windows since Declan had put the cop siren on the roof of his vehicle. She had her brother on FaceTime, trying to calm him while keeping a visual on Rosie.

Because truth be told, she was worried. Really worried. Rosie's muzzle was swelling so much the end of her nose was as wide as her face. "Hang on, Rory. We're only a couple of minutes away."

"Rosie's face is swelling up really bad." He cradled the dog in his arms, pacing around the kitchen. "I don't know what to do."

"I'm checking Google. Hold on." She pulled up the search engine, careful not to disconnect the call.

Declan stayed silent and focused beside her, taking the turns with speed and care, his experience in the cop car apparent. At a sharp bend in the road, a coffee thermos rolled in the floorboards and his dog tags hanging from the rearview mirror swayed in and out of her line of sight, but he never lost any degree of control.

Scrolling through the article on her phone, Charlotte searched for best tips to give Rory. "If you can see the stingers, pull them out."

"Rosie's really upset and wriggling. I don't know if I can..." Pausing, her brother sat on the floor, parting fur with one hand while petting the dog in soothing strokes with the other. "Okay, got one. Working on the others. Rosie, you're gonna be alright. Just be still. I've got you..."

His voice was so sweet and worried, her heart melted. This was her baby brother that she remembered. He was in there underneath all that hurt and anger. "You're doing great, Rory. Once you've finished that, get some ice and hold it against the swelling. If she won't let you do that, then get a very cold wet cloth and use that instead."

"I'm on it. But keep driving fast—" His jaw quivered. "Charlotte, she's gasping. I think her throat is closing up."

"Rory?" Declan called from behind the wheel. "We're turning on the road to your cabin. Be ready to pass over Rosie so we can take her to the emergency vet clinic. It's going to be okay."

Charlotte's hands shook as she searched for the information on the closest open veterinary hospital. Declan floored the accelerator, his jaw set, steady, dependable. There for her in a crisis.

And she knew without question, he wouldn't bail on her and the baby. She was grateful for that certainty for their child, especially when so much of her world was upside down right now. Declan would support her and their baby. But she also knew she needed—deserved—to be more than an obligation.

Declan had never owned a pet, but as he sat in the waiting room at the emergency vet clinic, he had to admit his heart was torn up with worry for little Rosie. Charlotte had called ahead to the emergency clinic from her car. Her voice had been steady but her hands shook as she cradled Rosie in her lap, the dog's eyes and nose so swollen she wheezed with every breath.

Once they'd arrived at the clinic, the veterinarian and a technician had rushed out to scoop the dog from her arms. Charlotte had been instructed to check in with the receptionist and wait in the lobby.

That had been twenty minutes ago. Twenty interminable minutes.

He'd done one of the grounding techniques he'd learned about from one of the dude ranch workshops and had counted all the right angles in a space. It's how he now knew that in the tree mural, there were twenty-five right angles. The birds soaring above the tree mural offered another five right angles.

Normally, this particular exercise calmed him. Today, though? The thudding in his chest continued to ricochet through him even as he focused his attention on the floating shelves sporting prescription dog and cat food.

He had been surprised Rory wanted to go with them to the emergency clinic. Declan had assumed the boy would welcome the chance to stay home alone. Or to roam free. But the teen had jumped right into the SUV to go with them. He wasn't talking much—slumped in a chair in a far corner of the waiting room, texting—but he was present.

Standing, Rory put away his phone and said, "I'm gonna get something to eat from the burger joint next door. Do you want anything?"

Charlotte shook her head. "I appreciate the offer, though."

Declan reached for his wallet and passed over a twenty-dollar bill.

"Thanks, Sheriff," Rory said before shuffling toward the front door, moving past a couple who had walked in with a parakeet in a cage. From beyond the green door, a dog barked three times.

Charlotte sagged back in the wooden bench, eyes skimming over the other folks in the waiting room. "I know I've only had Rosie for a couple of months, but I've grown really attached to her."

"Of course you have." He clasped her hand. "She's a sweet little dog."

Tears sheened in her sad blue eyes. "I just can't imagine having to tell her first owner that I let something happen to her."

"You didn't 'let' this happen. It was just an accident." He squeezed her hand and kissed the back of it before letting go, only to immediately miss the connection.

"I know, but…"

Then he realized what she'd said, about telling the first owner. "You know who had Rosie before? I thought you told me you adopted her from the shelter."

"I did," she clarified, sweeping back her hair from her face, "but it's more complicated than that."

"If you want to share, I'm listening. I have nowhere I'd rather be than here with you." The moment the words left his mouth, he felt the air change between them.

Charged with tension. And something more, joined in this moment of worry. How often might they find themselves in this same position down the road once they had an infant to care for?

Clearing her throat, she looked down and away. "I was visiting my mother. Her new roommate at the facility, an elderly lady, was upset because she couldn't keep her dog." Her forehead furrowed and she rubbed her sternum, as if relieving an ache. "So upset, she was having a panic attack and needed sedating. It was awful to see her dealing with such pain and helplessness."

"That's understandable," he said softly.

Charlotte's lips pursed tight before she continued, "I learned that the woman's family didn't want Rosie so they dumped her at a shelter." Anger laced her words. "Even knowing at nine years old her chances of being adopted were low."

"How did you find out?" He envisioned her at the facility, visiting her mom and getting embroiled in a whole other drama even when her plate was full to overflowing.

Charlotte was good like that. Tenderhearted and caring. He stroked his thumb over the back of her hand.

"The staff told me." Her face took on a faraway look, pain creasing her face. "The whole scene was awful. It stirred my mother up as well. Mom started crying, begging to go home so she could adopt the dog herself. But she's suicidal and until she's no longer a danger to herself, she has to stay. That's when I decided I had to save Rosie. It felt like the least I could do. I couldn't help Mom's roommate and I certainly can't do anything to help my mother."

He'd been through some tough scenes with his mom, but nothing like that. He'd always known his mother's troubles were tied into bad luck, but even when she was sad, she was always driven to right their ship. "How often do you get to see her?"

Inching her hand away, Charlotte picked at her

short nails. "We're allowed one visit a week, but most times she cancels."

"Aw, man, Charlotte. That's awful for you and for Rory." Even at her lowest times, no matter where he'd landed in the foster care system, his mother had called him every day. Even if she had to beg the use of someone else's cell phone.

"He doesn't go often. It's still too much for him." Her gaze skated toward the door, the fast-food joint visible through the glass panes. "Rory was the one who found our mother. She'd taken every pill in the house and lain down on her bed to die."

Sadness for her—for Rory—sucker punched him. He'd been on enough suicide-risk calls in his job to envision the scene. He rubbed over the tightness in his chest. "Tonight's scare with Rosie must have brought up a lot of bad stuff for him too."

A shuddering sigh wracked through her. "And just when I felt like he was making progress. Maybe I should talk to a counselor about my brother. I've mentioned it to him before, but he freaked out thinking I was accusing him of being like mom."

"Are you worried about that?"

She took her time answering, toying with the hem on her shirt. "I'm more worried about the impact of Mom's struggles on Rory. And I feel so clueless when dealing with him."

Declan slung his arm around her shoulders and pulled her in close until she rested her head on his shoulder. He wished he had the right words to offer, but sometimes in life, there just were just some things that couldn't be made better. All he could do was be present.

Palming the back of her head, he massaged his fingers through her hair, letting her silent tears soak his shirt. Time slipped into a sort of fugue, until he heard a voice call Charlotte's name.

The vet—a woman with kind eyes wearing paw-print scrubs—walked toward them, squatting in front of Charlotte.

"Miss Pace? Rosie's doing much better."

Charlotte sagged against Declan, her breath hitching on a sob.

"We were able to reverse the reaction with a hefty dose of antihistamines. She's breathing fine now. But I'd like to keep her overnight for observation—just as a precaution, given her age."

"Thank you, Doctor," Charlotte said, shooting to her feet. "Can we see her before we go?"

"Absolutely."

We? He would have thought that was a slip or that she meant Rory, until Charlotte looked back over her shoulder and held out her hand to him. Without hesitation, he went with her, unable to deny that the surge of protectiveness he felt around her grew stronger each day. And it had nothing to do with their baby.

Charlotte could hardly believe only an hour had passed since she and Declan had gone back to see Rosie, who'd been sedated and was sleeping in a soft dog bed right by the vet's desk. The relief she felt was still overwhelming.

And it felt like weeks since they had left for the dinner party at the Barnett house.

Now, Rory was upstairs with the rest of his fast food. He'd said he was exhausted—he'd sure looked wiped out—and that he was going to sleep. And while she didn't know what she wanted from this night, she knew she wasn't ready to say goodbye to Declan. She needed his steady, strong presence. Consequences could wait to be dealt with on another day.

So she'd invited him to stay.

They could sit in the yard by the chimenea and have the dessert they'd missed earlier. Nothing fancy. Just bottled water and a couple of brownies with peanut butter frosting. But she needed to decompress after the scare with her dog, and she had the feeling Declan could use the chance to wind down too.

Bent over the chimenea, his broad sculpted back to her, Declan meticulously started a fire. Warm embers glowed, giving way to dancing flames as he carefully added kindling. Night air brought forth a metronome of frog croaks and distant guitar chords from the rodeo arena. She placed the two plates and two bottles on the end table between the Adirondack chairs.

He glanced over his shoulder, smiled his thanks and then dropped into a seat. "Do you want me to go with you to get Rosie tomorrow? I'm free after work. Rory could come, too. We can get takeout… or ice cream, if that's what you're craving."

"*Craving?* Hmm." That word brought to mind memories of their kiss earlier. "I haven't really started having food cravings yet. I'm just glad not to be sick all the time. I do take the most amazing naps, though. It's almost like a coma. Crazy how a baby about the size of a chicken nugget can have so much control over my body."

"Is that a yes to us picking up Rosie together?" He lifted the brownie to his mouth.

"Yes, thank you. I appreciate your including Rory." Times like these it was tough to recall how angry she'd been when Declan broke up with her. A familiar tightening in her chest as she inhaled the crackling fire scent of burning oak.

"Of course I would want Rory along," he said without hesitation. "I meant it when I said I'm here for the kid."

Declan had a way with Rory, somehow peeling away the defensiveness. He had a knack for getting through to her brother that she envied.

Charlotte rolled the cool water bottle between her palms while she watched the flames dance. "You must have made quite an impact on those kids you taught during your Guard duty."

He shrugged off the compliment as he set the brownie back down on the plate. "It was mostly crowd control and rolling out the lesson plans the school provided. But we had some time for life conversations, too."

"Will you share with me about your teenage years?" she asked, needing to know more about him. Maybe because of how she'd opened up earlier. She didn't want things to be one-sided between them. They needed equal footing.

In response, his jaw tensed and flexed, his face in shadows as leaned back in the chair.

"Hey, I told you about my mom." She tapped her foot against his, nudging him to continue. "You can talk to me, too. We're tied through this little chicken nugget we made." Her hands covered her stomach, the curve just starting.

"We are, aren't we?" He reached toward her. "May I?"

A wad of emotion clogged her throat. How silly to worry about him touching her stomach when his hands had stroked every inch of her. Still, this felt far more intimate.

But this was his child and he wanted to connect. Who was she to deny him that?

Nodding, she moved her hands away, waiting, anticipating. He pressed his palm to her belly and she wished she could read his thoughts. His face was inscrutable, his head tucked. Then he looked up at her, awe in his chocolate brown eyes.

"Incredible." His voice was gravelly with emotion. "Even more than the ultrasound."

She placed her hand over his for a moment. "I

know you didn't want children. Please understand that I didn't plan this."

"I never thought you did." He slid his hand from under hers and palmed her cheek. "You're the most honest, honorable person I've ever met. It's a part of what drew me to you in the first place."

The dark of night added an air of privacy, the moonlight creating their own hazy bubble of illumination. How easy it would be to sink back into his arms.

But she'd had a purpose in launching this conversation and she intended to see it through. She leaned back in her chair until he withdrew his arm. "I'd like to hear about your months with the teens. Surely there was more than just lesson plans and crowd control," Charlotte said. "You taught civics and history, right? Was there room to add any of your own spin to the lessons?"

"Well, we had some extra time after a lesson on World War I," he said with a smile, absentmindedly peeling the label from the water bottle. "So I had them flip their desks, wad up paper and launch the wads at each other—as an example of trench warfare."

"Wow, that sounds incredible—and memorable." She was impressed. "I sure would have loved a lesson like that. I bet they enjoyed it."

"They did." He hitched one booted foot over his knee. "Then when we got to World War II, we put a shoebox wall down the middle of the class as an example of the Berlin Wall. Kids had to get a pass to go from one side to the other."

"I bet that made an impression," she said, prodding him along, hoping he would continue if she kept her answers short and encouraging.

"Once they realized they wouldn't be able to hang out with some of their friends, they got upset. Which led to some great discussions." He rubbed the back of his neck, his smile fading. "There were days I actually thought I was getting through to them."

"Thought?"

He pushed aside the plate of half-eaten brownie as if he'd lost his appetite. "Near the end of my time there, a couple of the kids in my third-period history class had a shootout in the parking lot of a fast-food restaurant."

"Oh no." She gasped, horrified—for the students and for him. She couldn't even begin to imagine. "That's awful. What happened to them? I hope no one…died?"

He glanced over at her quickly. "The two shooters both ended up in the hospital. One caught a bullet in the shoulder. The other lost a quarter of his intestines. When I joined up, I understood I might know people who got shot, but this wasn't what I expected." His chest rose and fell with a hefty breath. "Every class the whole time I was there, I told them all that they could come to me with any worries or fears. Yet neither of them breathed a word of anything that was going on between them. As a cop, I should know it's more complex than just asking for their trust."

"It's not wrong to hope." She rested a hand lightly on his elbow.

He leaned back in his chair, looking up toward the stars just visible between the branches. "I saw my first dead body when I was six."

She held herself very still, both too stunned to respond and also afraid if she spoke or moved, then the moment would be gone. He would close off the deeper parts of himself.

His thumbs scratched along the arms of the chair, digging deeper and deeper. "My mom and I were visiting her mother. Actually, *visiting* isn't the right word. We'd been evicted," he said, his voice emotionless in spite of the darkness of the memory he shared. "We were going to move in with Granny for the time being. Her place didn't have a spare room, but Mom said she would sleep on the sofa and I could sleep on the floor in Granny's room."

He painted a vivid picture in spite of the simple words and calm voice. Maybe because the stripped-down nature of the story left nothing but the cold, hard reality.

Scrubbing a hand over his jaw, he continued, "By the end of the week, gunshots woke me up in the middle of the night. I ran to the window to look. Granny hauled me down, but not in time. I'd already seen it. The body."

Her heart broke for that little boy then, and the

man he'd become now. A man who worked so tirelessly to save others. "No one should see that. Certainly not a child."

"Here's the thing." He met her gaze full on again, his eyes defiant, as if challenging her not to give an iota of sympathy. "That was probably one of the safer places we ever lived."

She didn't even know where to begin with the questions triggered by that statement. She sensed she needed to tread warily or he would shut down on her. "How much longer after that before you went into foster care?"

"My first placement was when I was in second grade," he said, picking up her hand again, stroking the inside of her wrist like a talisman. "The food was better, the houses were bigger, and I know it was the right place to be, given my mother's problems with money. But it wasn't home."

Finally, she thought she understood where he was going with sharing this memory. "Are you saying that's how Rory feels? Like he's not home?"

"The opposite, actually. At Granny's, I still felt like I was home, regardless of how bad things got. You're home for Rory." He gave a wry grin, but the shadowy pain of his memory still lurked in his brown eyes. "And the dude ranch is far from a bad place to land."

Hearing the suffering he'd been through—the loss, the turmoil—and seeing the man he'd become, how he'd pulled all that together to build a life of service, tugged at her every heartstring at a time when her emotions were already close to the surface. Especially when the kiss they'd shared in the SUV was still so fresh in her mind, tingling just under the surface.

Her defenses had been weakening ever since the scare with Rosie, her appreciation for Declan growing. Now, after he'd trusted her with the story of his difficult past, she felt the last of her boundaries fall.

Without hesitation or regret, she rose from her chair and into his lap. Taking advantage of the surprise holding him still, she slid her arms around his neck and pressed her mouth to his.

Chapter Ten

Declan's brain went offline the second Charlotte dropped into his lap and kissed him.

But once he gathered his scrambled thoughts, he was all in. He tunneled his fingers into her hair and drew her closer. His eyes closed, blocking out even the dim moonlight and immersing him in just sensation.

The scent of lavender clinging to her mixing with the smokiness in the air from the firepit. The feel of her in his arms was familiar but new all at once. The taste of her on his tongue, he remembered well, especially in his dreams. The silkiness of her skin was like balm to his soul. Her curves, however, were subtly different. Her breasts were fuller, and, of course, her stomach bore the slightest of bumps where they'd started their family together.

Family?

His mind shied away from the word and focused fully on this moment, with Charlotte. Even if it was just a kiss and nothing more, he didn't intend to take privilege of that for granted ever again.

As their embrace grew more intense, he began to wonder if she wanted more than just kisses tonight. Or was that just very hopeful thinking on his part?

Trailing her fingers along his jawline, she broke their kiss and stared at him with passion-filled blue eyes. "Can we agree that for the next few hours we won't think about the past or the future, focus instead on just this…incredible chemistry we have?"

Excitement leaped in his veins, urging him to stop talking and scoop her up, but still, he had to ask, "Are you sure this is alright with you? I don't want to presume or for us to have regrets."

"I'm certain." She placed her hands on either side of his face, moonlight streaming over her blond hair. "I'm *beyond* certain that I want to be with you tonight."

"What about Rory?" He didn't want to cause friction with the boy.

She glanced up to his bedroom window on the second floor. The light was out. Apparently, Rory was every bit as tired as he'd said—and appeared—when they'd returned from the emergency vet clinic.

Looking back down at him, Charlotte slid her hands from his face to his chest. "Would you mind leaving before he wakes up in the morning? I don't want to make his life any more confusing."

"Understood—and agreed." He touched a finger to her lips and traced the cupid's bow outline. "Do you mind if I hold you after until you fall asleep?"

"I would love that," she said with a seductive gleam in her eyes. "But you know what I would love even more right now?"

Anticipation crackled like a lightning strike along his skin. "What would that be?"

She grabbed a fistful of his shirt and tugged him with her toward the steps. "For us to ditch all of these clothes and for you to make me forget about the rest of the world for a few hours."

"Challenge accepted." He shot to his feet and hooked one arm around her waist, pulling her to him.

Arching up on her toes, she whispered along his cheek, "And we'll need to be very quiet."

He kissed the line of her throat, then growled against her lips, "I can think of plenty of ways for us to silence each other."

Crazy how a kiss could muddle a mind. Or rather kisses from this particular woman. Their legs tangled in a dance of desire as they made their way across the yard, sidestepping the garden on the way to the porch. Laughing softly together, they made fast tracks up the steps.

Easing back from him, she opened the door and peered inside. No sign of Rory and no light streaming from under his bedroom door.

Declan was free to focus completely on making the most of this night with Charlotte.

Walking silently, she clasped his hand and led him toward her bedroom. He'd been there before, but this felt like a first for them. Certainly, everything had changed since the last time they were together. That rendezvous had included a romantic evening skinny-dipping in the Sulis Springs cave. The memory of the encounter wrapped around him, making him nostalgic for a time when things between them had been less complicated.

Or rather, for a time when they'd both been content not to delve deeper. Not to share all those worries and demons.

"Declan? Are you okay?" She tugged his hand, drawing his attention back to the here and now.

"Yes, ma'am, I'm all yours," he said with a smile.

She closed the door and sealed them inside with her brass bed and inviting floral comforter. The space was pretty and soft, like Charlotte, full of flowers and beautiful scents.

One step deeper into the room and frenzy took hold of him. Of her as well. He swept aside her clothes as quickly as she dispatched his, flinging each piece aside until a pile formed in a corner. And then they were standing together in the middle of the floor, braided rug under their bare feet.

They stood flesh to naked flesh. He pressed a hand to her stomach. While he'd done the same earlier, it felt completely different with no barriers between them. A surge of protectiveness hammered through him. For their child. For her. He was overtaken by a need to claim them as his own.

Smiling her encouragement, she backed toward the bed, drawing him with her. He reclined her onto the poofy comforter, covering her with his body only to have her urge him to lie under her. Charlotte straddled him, an incredible vision with her blond hair streaming over her shoulders.

And as he lost himself in the sensation and beauty of her, he could almost believe there was a way for them to be together. That he could set aside all those worries about falling short of what she deserved.

Her body languid and sated, Charlotte stretched her hand out across the bed…only to find it empty. The sheets had long gone cold. Declan must have left her hours ago. She tried not to feel sad about it, knowing it was what she had asked. And anyway, she had lovely memories to keep her company. She'd fallen asleep in his arms after they made love. Their chemistry had been even stronger than she remembered.

How long had she been drowsing?

Rolling to her back, she blinked until her eyes accommodated the dark. She reached on her bedside table for her cell phone to check the time… Only four. While she wanted Declan beside her, at least she could stay in bed a while longer, wrapped in the reminiscence of being together earlier. She wasn't sure what it meant or where it would lead, but she didn't have to come up with those answers just yet.

For now, she could savor the memory of making love with Declan again. It had been so long, months, since their date night alone in the ranch's Sulis Spring cave, complete with dinner followed by dipping into the hot springs. The evening had been fairy-tale perfect, and decadent in a way beyond what either of them could normally have afforded, but there were many perks of working at the Top Dog Dude Ranch—including vouchers to use on some of the facilities when they weren't reserved by other guests.

She closed her eyes and sank back into her pillow, the scent of him still lingering to the sheets, to her skin…

Charlotte sank deeper into the churning waters of the Sulis Springs cave, the scent of sulfur tingeing the air. Her body soaked in the warmth, leaving her languid.

Or maybe that was from the sexy sheriff occupying the waters with her. Just the two of them. Alone. No demands of the outside world.

The bubbling hot springs they occupied offered healing on both a physical and spiritual level, providing a holistic experience. And right now, Charlotte needed everything the famed springs had to offer. Helping set up for a bridal shower there earlier in the day had made her realize there was an open slot in the schedule tonight—a rarity.

Cave walls were periodically painted by guests in art therapy classes, the images depicting their history, joys and pains. Pottery also lined the walls, pieces created by all ages. Candles were arranged around the water's edge and classical music echoed softly from her cell phone.

She was struggling to balance among work, her new relationship with Declan and keeping Rory from setting his world on fire. She understood her brother was hurt by a long history of bad memories with their mother and father. Her parents' defection had hit him in ways that she couldn't have predicted, but she was doing her best to be supportive. And while she carried those heartaches from their broken family as well, she was an adult. She just hoped she was adult enough to do right by her sibling at this crucial time in his young life.

Thank goodness Declan had been working around her crazy schedule as best he could. Her heart leaped as she took in the sight of him swimming closer, his muscled arms slicing through the water. Steam rose around him. She could hardly believe she'd pulled this off—an evening's romantic getaway with Declan.

Tonight, they'd taken their relationship to the next level. Her body still tingled in the aftermath of making love in the cave, such a beautifully romantic setting.

Extending a hand to him, she tugged him to sit be-

side her on the rock ledge seat in the springs. "You're too far away," she teased. "I miss you."

He grasped her by the waist and pulled her to straddle his lap. "Hello, gorgeous. I've missed you, too. It's been at least three minutes since I touched you."

His gravelly voice rumbled his chest against hers.

She stroked back a damp lock from his forehead. "Thank you for meeting me here."

"Thank you for being you." He angled a kiss over her mouth, his broad palms against her waist. "I hope you know how incredible you are. This evening with you... It's been..." He paused, whistling low.

She couldn't agree more. Their chemistry when making love had blindsided her. Already her body hummed for more. Soon. She wanted the evening to last. He'd brought a picnic. She'd supplied a thick quilt.

"I'm sorry we have to sneak around so much for time alone. I'm just not comfortable having you sleep over because of Rory. I know we're adults, and we don't owe anyone an explanation, but..." She wanted to avoid anything that caused more controversy with her brother. The fights between them were already difficult enough.

"Say no more. He's a teenager." His smile faded and he shifted her from his lap to her seat beside him again. "Trust me, I understand."

His arm slid around her shoulders and she nes-

tled against him. "It's a scary responsibility, looking out for him."

"Rory doesn't make it easy," he said wryly.

No kidding. "I appreciate your help with him. You set such a powerful example of a successful, strong man."

He tensed for a moment, then smiled. Stroking her face, fingers tunneling into her hair, he said, "Flattery will get you everywhere."

"That's my hope." She wriggled against him.

Chuckling, he slipped his arms around her and stood, water sheeting from their bodies as he walked up the stone steps toward their quilt and dinner. Towels were folded by the picnic basket, the perfect date waiting to be enjoyed with the perfect man. As they neared the blanket, he set her down. Their fingers linked, she playfully drew him with her.

From a few feet away, resting on her discarded clothes, her phone chimed with an incoming text. A reminder of real life and all the problems she'd wanted to leave behind when she entered the cave tonight. The tug-of-war going on inside her strengthened—her job, her brother, her growing feelings for this man—all pulling at her and she didn't have a clue how to keep it from tearing her apart as alarm bells echoed through her...

Charlotte startled awake, the sound of her phone alarm piercing through her sleep, through her dream. Except it wasn't really a dream. More of a memory that had bled through into slumber. She'd been so full of hope for her relationship with Declan then, before he'd broken her heart.

To be fair to him, he'd been honest with her from the start, making it clear that he was committed to his job to the exclusion of everything else. Somehow, though, she'd deluded herself that he would change his mind. He was so giving of himself to others, after all.

She hadn't realized there was a wall around his heart until she ran smack dab into it.

And she would be wise to remember that now more than ever. Because she didn't have the option of simply cutting him out of her life anymore. They had a child together, which meant she needed to keep a close watch over her own heart.

Starting today.

Sweeping aside the covers, she placed her feet on the cool morning floor, determined that she and Declan would have to set some very firm ground rules before even entertaining the notion of resuming their relationship.

Last night, Rory had slept like a rock.

Not just because they'd stayed up late at the vet clinic, but because worry was exhausting. Thank goodness Rosie was okay. He'd been scared, more afraid than he could ever remember.

Scrappy Rosie looked none the worse for wear, thank goodness. She lay beside him on the blanket, chewing a toy. She'd even hobbled around the yard a little bit—staying well clear of the bushes where she'd been swarmed by bees.

If only he could be as smart as Rosie. But instead, here he was, at loose ends wishing he could figure out a way to hang out with Olivia. Even though he knew she would be leaving before long, he still wanted to make the most of the time she had left at the ranch.

Provided she even wanted to see him. He was starting to wonder if she might be avoiding him after what her friends had revealed.

The sense of being watched creeped over him, stopping his thoughts short. He glanced up to find Olivia leaning on the picket fence around his cabin.

As if conjured by his thoughts.

Her hands on the wooden posts, she made a pretty picture in jean shorts and a pullover sweatshirt bearing the ranch's paw print-horseshoe logo. She flipped her glossy black ponytail over her shoulder with a twitch of her head. "Hey, do you mind if I join you?"

Seriously? Of course he didn't mind. But he didn't want to look too eager. He grabbed Rosie's tennis ball and tossed it a few feet away. "Aren't you supposed to be on vacation?"

"I told my parents I was going to lunch with Zoey and Corrine," she said, stepping toward the gate, trailing her fingers along the top of the fence. "My friends said they would cover for me to come visit you. I was heading to the stables when I saw you here."

Wow, so they didn't think less of him after all. That was a relief.

He looked back at the cabin. His sister was inside, but she probably wouldn't care as long as they stayed outside. It wasn't like he was taking a girl up to his bedroom. "Sure, come on."

A smile lit her whole face as she swung the gate wide, careful to close it and latch it behind her so Rosie couldn't slip out. She crossed to the tire swing hanging from a tree beside him and sat, tapping her toe in the dirt to start a slow sway.

Standing, he shifted into an Adirondack chair closer to her and searched for something to say. "Cool pullover." Wow, how stupid was that of a comment? "I saw you wearing a junior orchestra shirt one day. Was that yours?"

"Yeah, I play the flute. I got the instrument as a hand-me-down from a cousin." Olivia played with the ends of her glossy ponytail, eyes cast downward and hidden by the sweep of her long lashes. "I wanted to play the trumpet, but instruments are expensive. It's okay, though. I'm just glad to get to play."

"What kind of music do you—"

The creak of the screen door cut the air and he looked up to see his sister walking onto the porch, balancing a tray full of food. "Rory, I brought you out a bite to eat for lunch. There's enough for both of you. Nothing fancy. A couple of pimento cheese sandwiches, some chips and soda. Cookies too."

His sister placed the tray on the table between

the Adirondack chairs. Definitely more than enough food. Rory wondered if she'd planned to eat with him. Sweet of her to make his—friend? girlfriend?—feel welcome.

Olivia stood, swiping the wrinkles from her jean shorts. "Thanks, Miss Pace, this looks really great."

Kneeling, Charlotte clapped her hands for Rosie to toddle over. "I'll take Rosie so you can talk."

"Wait," Rory said before thinking. "If it's okay with you, I'll keep her. I'll make sure she rests and I've been keeping her bowl refilled with fresh water."

"Of course she can stay outside." Charlotte pushed her hands against her knees as she stood. "She'll enjoy it."

Charlotte tucked her hands into the pockets of her canvas apron, which she had embroidered with daisies. He could have sworn his sister winked at him before turning on her heel. The door creaked open and then he heard the click signifying it had been pulled shut. A sheepish grin plastered to his face as he turned his attention back to Olivia.

Dropping into the seat next to him, Olivia popped open a soda can. Sounds of fizzing bubbles filled the momentary silence. "Your sister is nice."

"Yeah, she really is." He wasn't sure why he was so cranky to her all the time. It was like he couldn't help himself. "It was good of her to take me in when our mom got sick."

"With tuberculosis, right?" Olivia picked up a

double chocolate chip cookie and broke off a piece, popping it in her mouth.

"Uh, actually, I didn't tell the truth about that. I was embarrassed." He paused, dropping his hand for Rosie to join him. The pup trotted over, nudged his hand and then curled into a ball on the grass. It was hard not being able to talk about it with his friends Truitt and Kai, for fear they would think he was like his mother. But something made him think it would be easier to tell Olivia, especially since she'd still come around even after what her friends revealed. "Mom had some kind of nervous breakdown. She's in a hospital until they're sure she won't hurt herself."

The second the words were out of his mouth, he felt like a weight had been lifted.

"That's rough. I'm really sorry." Her deep brown eyes met his with warmth for a moment before she looked away and took another nibble of her cookie. "Will you go back to live with her when she gets discharged?"

No judgment from Olivia. Just sympathy. He never would have gotten that from his friends. But could he really call them friends? Kai and Truitt had stopped coming around to see him since the gift shop mess, even though he knew from social media that they'd gotten burgers and gone to a movie last night.

Shaking his head, he hauled his focus back to Olivia's question, his fingers lightly stroking Rosie's soft fur. "I suppose I could go back to Mom's when she's out. I mean, I miss her. But I'm not sure Charlotte will allow it. She says Mom's not able to take care of me."

Olivia popped the last bite into her mouth, her eyebrows pinching together in thought as she chewed. "I know this kinda isn't the same, but it sorta is. I'm not sure where I'll be living when my parents split up. I hate not knowing."

Her hands were clasped together all tight like, her knuckles white with a stress he knew well.

"It really is the same in the ways that matter." He passed her the bowl of chips. "It's good to have someone who understands."

Their hands grazed in the pass-off, her eyes going wide for an instant. "Do you get to see your mom? Or talk to her?"

His hands dropped to his lap again, his skin still warm from where they'd touched. "Sometimes. Not a lot, though. Everybody was always giving me BS answers about why it won't work out even after we made the drive over. So I just stopped going at all."

"Where is she?" Olivia asked.

Averting his gaze, he picked up a pimento cheese sandwich, fingers sinking into the plump bread, with the crust all cut off like their mom always made. Taking a deep breath, he swallowed. "In a facility over in Gatlinburg. That's actually how we got Rosie. Another patient there had to give her up. It was really sad."

Rosie stretched and yawned, then walked under the chair to enjoy a shady place to sleep. The lady who'd had her before had given them a letter with a list with her routine and all her favorite toys. He'd never asked why that woman was there. It was hard enough knowing why his mom was in that place.

He'd never forget what she'd looked like when he'd found her. Bile burned his throat and he struggled to swallow it back down.

"Gatlinburg's not so far from Moonlight Ridge." Olivia reached over and squeezed his arm. "Perhaps we could go see the lady who used to have your dog. We could show her pictures of Rosie and tell her how good she's doing—well, other than the bee-sting thing. While we're there, you could see your mom too."

"We?" His brain was scrambled by the feel of her touching him. He crunched a chip and wondered if his heart was as loud as the chewing sounded. It sure felt that way. "Together? But how would we get there?"

"I can take my parents' car." Her voice picked up speed with excitement even as she kept her volume low, glancing at the porch and back quickly. "I have my driver's license. I'll just tell them I'm heading into Moonlight Ridge for something. Zoey and Corrine would cover for us. I know they would."

He turned the thought over in his brain for a moment, still feeling guilty for what happened to Rosie. When all those stings happened, she must have especially missed her first mom. Maybe after the visit he could even talk about a way to arrange for Rosie to come too sometime… Still, though, he worried about upsetting Charlotte.

"I don't know. My sister has really been on me about accountability and stuff." Even as he said it, though, he really wanted to go with Olivia. The thought of being with her in the car was exciting.

And knowing she cared enough about him to help him see his mother? That meant a lot to a guy who didn't feel special in anybody's world. "You know, the lady who had Rosie is actually my mom's roommate."

"That makes it even more convenient." Olivia folded her legs crisscross.

He caught a whiff of her vanilla-scented perfume as she leaned closer. Her knee brushed against his with a featherlight touch. The whisper of her touch felt electric. "I know the lady would be glad to have an update."

"I think taking Rosie would make the perfect excuse to go and no way could my mom or the staff say no. We're doing a good thing for the roommate and for Rosie. If for some reason they don't let Rosie in to visit, I can watch her while you go inside. You could bring the lady to the window and I'll hold Rosie up. It'll be really cool."

Actually take Rosie? Now?

That could work. And if he went because of the dog, there wouldn't be so much pressure on him or his mom to have some perfect visit. After those first two times he'd come up there, she'd canceled every time he was with Charlotte. It was still hard, thinking about what she'd tried to do. He was probably a big reminder too, since he was the one who found her.

Could that be why she kept canceling on seeing them?

Maybe.

Did she blame him for saving her?

That thought hurt. A lot. But while seeing each other might be tough, he was starting to think that too much time apart was making the anticipation of it worse, like flinching over tugging off a band aid.

And he missed her. His mother.

Dropping a hand to pet Rosie, he drew in a ragged breath as determination grew inside him. He was going to see his mom. He just had to figure out how to ditch stable duty without Charlotte and Declan catching him. Charlotte would probably find out later whenever she learned about his visit, but he would figure out a way to smooth that over later. Or take his latest punishment.

Because nobody was going to stop him.

Chapter Eleven

Seated at his office desk, Declan scrolled through the report on his computer, draining the last of his fourth cup of java. Late day sun streamed through his office window, while outside the parking lot bustled with the activity of the others leaving work. He'd been restless after leaving Charlotte, his mind full of images of her curled up in bed.

Going home to his empty studio apartment hadn't sounded appealing so he'd detoured to work instead, figuring if he needed to catch a catnap he could use the sofa across from his desk instead. He'd made use of that couch so often after working late he figured he'd left a permanent imprint in the well-worn leather.

One good thing about his lack of sleep? He'd

caught up on every piece of work that had piled up during his time away for the Guard.

Restoring order to his life through his chosen profession usually settled the restlessness deep inside him. No such luck today, because he couldn't shake the sense that Charlotte didn't intend for last night's connection to continue long term.

And for him? He was back to his original thought that they should move in together. The sooner the better. Trying to keep things platonic hadn't helped, and in fact had brought more stress. All his reasons for walking away before were invalid now that they had a baby on the way.

Drawing in a deep breath, he creaked back in his office chair, welcoming the clarity of thought this space brought. Something about working in a renovated and converted hundred-year-old train station felt peaceful, timeless. It was soothing to take in the red brick of the walls where so many people had come and gone before him, all on their way to something. The place felt like a threshold between one world and the next.

He certainly had felt that way years ago when he hung his commission into the National Guard next to his bachelor's in criminal justice on the wall behind his desk. He'd felt like this job was that threshold space to a new life, one where he could make up for some of the hell-raising of his lonely youth.

Exhaling, he stacked some case notes into a crisp manila folder, and shut the books that had been splayed open, stacking them neatly in the corner. As he stood, his chair scraped against the hardwood floor. Swiping the Top Dog mug from his desk, he walked toward the black coffeepot and set the mug down beside it. Warm cinnamon scent tickled his nose as he walked out of his office. Before he and Charlotte had broken up months ago, she'd gifted him a diffuser and natural oils, scents made by her from her garden. It was a good memory, a reminder that their previous relationship was defined by more than just their breakup.

As he left his office, he clicked the door shut behind him and set out to the lobby. Bright sunlight filled the high ceiling with rafters. It was probably the most inviting police station to exist, not just because of the building's ambiance but also because of his secretary, Lorelei, a mother of seven and grandmother of twenty-three. The glue that held the office together, she'd been with the department since graduating from high school, and she was a real firecracker. He didn't know how he would ever manage around here without her.

"Lorelei, could you make sure any calls are forwarded to my cell?"

"You bet, Sheriff," she said, moving aside a stack of files, her grandma charm bracelet jingling with a personalized disc for each grandbaby. "I hope you're off to have some R & R. You were here before I arrived."

"Just doing the job the good people of Moonlight

Ridge elected me to do." He snagged his Stetson off the coatrack on his way toward the door.

"Given how much paperwork you've plowed through that now needs filing, they're getting more than their money's worth."

Chuckling, he waved on his way out, stepping onto the brick pavers that led to the parking lot with his SUV. As he walked, he tucked his hands into his coat jacket. This morning, the weather had been cool and crisp. Although the cloudless sky of the morning gave way into a warm spring afternoon.

"Declan?" a familiar feminine voice called out.

The sound of his name stopped him short. But then the sound of Charlotte's voice had a way of catching his attention more than any other.

Scanning, he found her sitting on a bench in the small park by the station's lot. Beautiful in a striped, loose sundress, her blond hair swept back by sunglasses on her head. She'd clearly been waiting for him. He took a moment to gauge her mood and found her to be determined—based on the set of her jaw—but not angry. He could work with that.

Spring birds flitted from nearby tree branches, singing when they landed in the safety of the leaves. Down the street, the town sparked to life while the small fountain in front of the bench gurgled a steady flow of clear water. Days like today made Declan feel so damn grateful he took a chance on this place.

"Well, hello, beautiful," he said, making fast tracks toward her, leaning down to press a lingering kiss on her lips, before sitting beside her. "What brings you here? Not that I'm complaining."

"We haven't had time to talk since last night, other than a couple of quick texts."

"Uh-huh," he said, stretching his arm along the bench. He'd sent her a text this morning, just a hello and asking her to supper.

She hadn't answered.

Charlotte crossed her legs at her ankles, her toes scrunching in her leather sandals. "I don't regret our time together last night."

Declan skimmed a finger along her bare arm, eyes momentarily flicking to the older couple who strode by hand in hand. The gentleman kissed his wife's hand as he gestured for her to sit down on a bench across from them. Something in Declan's chest tightened. "I sense a *but* coming."

"But," she said, proving him right, "we need to set some ground rules if we're going to see each other in the future." Her hand drifted to rest on his knee.

"You said *future*." He winked, needing to keep things light so she wouldn't feel pressured and bolt. A young kid whizzed by, running full out toward the park's playground. The kid's mom and dad, both dressed in athletic wear, jogged past them, trailing their eager son. Each family tableau strolling by reminding him of the stakes with Charlotte.

"Short term," she answered quickly, squeezing his knee. "Remember when we called a truce for the evening?"

"How could I forget?" he asked with a grin.

She drew in a deep breath, pausing until a shopper with an armload of packages hurried by along the sidewalk, then continued, "I propose that we call a truce until the May Day festival. We can act like we're a regular dating couple."

"I like what I'm hearing so far." He tucked her closer against his side and took heart when she didn't scoot away.

Her throat moved in a slow swallow as a family of four walked by, the father pushing the stroller with a toddler, the mother visibly pregnant. How simple it could be to have a life like that. To have a family built on trust and support. He never imagined a life like that, a family of his own, until Charlotte.

"Before you misunderstand..." She held up a hand. "I don't want to talk about the baby or the long-term future. I just want both of us take a breather and enjoy being together for now."

He hadn't expected to win this easily, but he was certainly glad to agree. Ironic, given the fact he hadn't been able to run from commitment fast enough a few short months ago. But even more than the connection of the baby, he wanted to be with her. He'd missed her during his Guard duty, more than he could have imagined. "I have a condition of my own."

"What would that be?" Her blue eyes narrowed suspiciously.

"It'll be more than sex." He tucked a knuckle under

her chin, his gaze holding hers. "We spend time together. And hopefully even figure out all those things we never got around to sharing before."

She gave him a wobbly smile, hand fluttering up to smooth his uniform collar. "Since we're linked forever, that makes sense."

Now that he'd made progress, he wasn't wasting another minute. "I'm finished with work for the day, so if you're free now too, I'd like to ask you out on a first date of our new start."

"I'd like that. Rory told me he's working overtime at the stables to finish his commitment faster. He even took Rosie with him so he can keep an eye on her."

"That's great." The boy really seemed to be making progress. "Dinner downtown? Or we could go into Gatlinburg."

"Actually, I was thinking, if you don't mind, there's a small concert in the park at the ranch. I can use one of my employee vouchers to attend. Raise the Woof is performing. There will even be dancing."

"Dancing? With you?" Standing, he extended his hand to her. "I'm all in."

The thought of holding her in his arms for the evening made his heart speed and his hopes rise. He'd been so certain she wouldn't budge on moving in together, but now? He was one step closer to his goal.

Worries about being worthy of her couldn't matter anymore. Because he wasn't giving up on Charlotte and their baby.

* * *

Charlotte couldn't remember when she'd had so many butterflies on a first date. But dancing under the stars in Declan's arms, she could almost forget all the worries about the future.

She was now a big fan of truces.

Twinkling string lights stretched amid the trees that framed the wooden outdoor dance floor. The lights looked like the stars above came down to earth, hovering close to maybe, just maybe, grant a wish to a hopeful dreamer. Her friend Eliza set a romantic tone with her keyboard. The drums and fiddle were being played by newlyweds who worked in the stables.

This slower song, a new breakout country single, afforded Charlotte a chance to take in Declan's handsome face, tanned from time outdoors, his bright eyes with crinkles at the corners. Gone was the sheriff's uniform.

Instead, when Declan pulled her close to his chest, her fingers pressed against the red plaid flannel that accented his well-built frame. His musky scent reassured her amid a crowd of fifty, making her believe for a moment the only two people in the whole world were the two of them. He'd been so amenable to her idea for a truce, so accommodating of her wish to delay thinking about the future. She really appreciated the emotional break from the stress. Especially with her worries about her brother.

For now, she just wanted to enjoy the warmth and strength of the man who held her close.

As they swayed, Declan's voice rumbled in his chest. "They're a talented group. Who's the new guy on the guitar?"

"That's Ian Greer. While you were away..." She bit her lip for an instant, the pain of that time apart threatening to tarnish the beauty of the night. Clearing her throat, she began again, "While you were away, the ranch acquired a partnership in a Christmas tree farm on the land the Greers have owned for generations. His mother has Alzheimer's and he needed money for her care. He was going to sell the whole place, but Jacob and Hollie worked out a partnership deal."

"They're good people." He nodded toward the O'Briens, who were standing by the open barn doors. Behind them, a dinner buffet was in full swing.

"We're already planning some events on the Christmas tree farm that will be open to the public, like our Harvest Festival parade. It'll be a holiday to remember." Her heart clenched at the realization this would be her baby's first Christmas. What kind of family traditions would they start? Her own had been so haphazard. "What's your favorite Christmas memory? Or is that not okay to ask? I wouldn't want to bring up unhappy memories."

Declan's warm hands skimmed her lower back as they danced. "You mean from foster care or juvie? Mom and I had some fun Christmas traditions on those holidays we spent together. We frosted cookies and put sprinkles on them. We would take walks and look at the Christmas lights."

"Cookies?" The answer was sweet and a surprise. "What kind? Sugar or gingerbread?"

"Both, actually." His deep brown eyes took on a nostalgic air, his hands moving hypnotically along the small of her back. "No matter how broke we were, she figured out a way to get me presents. She signed up for those angel tree giveaways at church."

Now that was a dose of reality. In spite of all her mom's struggles, they'd never had money troubles. Her accountant mother had been tight with a dollar. "I'm glad she was able to arrange that for you."

"I always thought it was messed up that they didn't do the angel tree in reverse so the kids could get gifts for their parents." He spun her deftly around the planked dance floor, glimpses of other couples laughing and clapping as the tempo increased. "Sure, they gave Mom gifts, but it wasn't the same. Not to me, at least."

"You loved your mom."

"I still do," he said with a smile. "This one Christmas, I really wanted to get something better for her than some lopsided pottery I'd made in art class. I went door to door asking for odd jobs, like mowing the grass. I made enough to get her perfume and a scarf."

"Please, please don't say this story has a sad ending, like your money getting stolen by a playground bully." She blinked back emotional tears over the image of him as a child, imagining what their little one would look like. "I don't think my hormones could handle it."

"No worries, nothing bad happened." He skimmed his mouth over hers. "She loved the perfume and wore the scarf to work every day for the rest of winter." His eyes took on a faraway look as if he could see those years gone by. "It felt really good to do something nice for her. I just wish I could have been a better son in my teenage years."

Her feet slowed and she cradled his face in her hands, drawing his gaze back to her. "You'll make up for it by being a better father to your child. You're already an incredible father figure to Rory."

His throat bobbed with a deep swallow. "Your trust means a lot to me, Charlotte. I'll do my best not to let you down."

She could see how hard he was trying. Still, this was new and scary territory for them. She needed to take her own advice and keep this truce light, no talk of the future.

So she arched up on her toes and kissed him to silence him. And yes, because she wanted to. She'd wanted Declan from the moment she'd seen him, and that feeling had only grown.

Declan eased back and she almost groaned aloud in disappointment. Until he clasped her hand and tugged lightly. "Let's move this date into the barn and grab something to eat. There are storm clouds gathering overhead."

Nodding, she slid her arm around his waist as they walked, and tried to tell herself those clouds weren't an omen.

Declan savored the feel of Charlotte's soft body pressed to his side as they raced toward the supper party in the barn to avoid the rain.

But even more than the feel of her, he reveled in the joy of declaring to their friends that they were a couple. When she had chosen a Top Dog event for their date, she had to have known the gossip mill would churn into high gear.

Already he could feel the eyes of their friends, the nods and knowing smiles. All good-natured. He'd never lived in one place long enough to have this many people who cared about his life.

A thought to mull over another day. Right now, he just wanted to focus on sharing a meal with Charlotte. They'd eaten together here at the ranch before, but they both knew this was different. The start of something new.

He shook the rain off his hat as she scavenged a scrunchie from her purse, then swept her damp hair back into a ponytail. Massive ceiling fans overhead stirred the air that was growing muggier by the moment.

They loaded their plates with Top Dog Ranch's world-famous barbecue chicken wings, fried pickles and salt-and-vinegar potato wedges. Declan's stomach grumbled as he cut across the barn to where a picnic table set for two was decorated with red checkered tablecloths and pretty sunflower centerpieces he would wager had been arranged by Charlotte. He admired her gift and dedication to her job.

He pointed to the smaller table. "Do you mind if we sit here?"

"It means no one will join us, so yes. Let's make this about the two of us." She skimmed her fingers along his hand, glancing to the nearby fiddle player set in the corner a few paces away. "Maybe I shouldn't have suggested we come here."

"Indulging in all the ranch has to offer is a treat. I appreciate our friends here. And it's probably best to be closer to Rory." Declan pulled out the seat for Charlotte, who blushed faintly. "Were you able to reach him?"

"Yes, thank goodness. I texted him and he said he's taking care of Rosie and not to worry." A slow song from the fiddle player fit the moody thunder still rumbling outside.

Declan popped a potato wedge in his mouth, the tangy taste of vinegar and salt tart along his tongue. "That's a relief. Sorry our dancing got cut short."

She reached to touch his knee. Electricity pulsed through him that could rival the storm's lightning. His right hand dropped to take her delicate fingers in his, her calluses from gardening a contrast to the silkiness of her skin…elsewhere.

"Declan, I hope you know I'm thankful for all the time you've spent with him lately."

"I don't want him to have to go through what I did to get his act together." Memories from his teen years tugged at him, of having no real direction, no hope. He still struggled with trusting the future.

"Do you mean the time you spent in juvie?" she asked softly.

The dim light in their shadowy corner added a layer of privacy, which he was grateful for. Good thing he hadn't chosen the corner near the vintage single-lane bowling alley and mechanical bull. The chaos of that corner wouldn't have afforded them this intimate conversation.

And he needed her to see how committed and serious he was.

"Yeah, it's rough in there, from the worst of the worst criminals all the way to kids in for truancy." He rubbed his thumb along the inside of her wrist, so soft, soothing the ragged edges of his nerves. "And we're all fighting for survival. Any infraction—like a fight—can add to your time."

"Did that happen to you?" She pushed aside her plate, her full attention on him.

He shook his head, throwing his napkin on top of the fried pickles, his appetite gone. "Those of us who stayed out of trouble got to participate in training programs—like woodwork, welding, even earning a forklift driver's license."

"Which did you choose?" she asked, eyeing him over the rim of her glass of sweet tea.

Rain pelted the tin roof, mixing with the whooping of the small crowd as a young woman tried her hand at the mechanical bull. No matter how hard he attempted to stay solely focused on the present space, his cop instincts ensured he always scanned the surroundings, taking interest in little movements, assessing potential threats.

Truth be told, that instinct had started as a teen, watching his back at every turn in his ever-changing life.

"Forklift driver. I wanted a job when I got out so I would have choices, good ones. And it worked. I was able to get a place of my own. It wasn't much, but I invited my mom to join me." He'd hoped to help her finally stabilize her life. "But she said it was my time."

He'd known she really meant she had a new boyfriend. Of course, that was her right and he wanted her to be happy. Still, it was tough to trust in her luck or judgment in the relationship department. Sure enough, she'd broken it off with that guy not long later, moving on to another equally underwhelming fellow who'd taken her car without asking and totaled it. Declan had bought her a used sedan, glad to be able to do something for her.

Charlotte linked her fingers with his and squeezed. "Like I said earlier. You're a good son. I'm sure the offer meant a lot to her."

He shrugged through a kink in his shoulders. Why was his mom on his mind so much? Probably because of facing parenthood himself and hoping he could do a better job than her. Because as much as he loved his mom, he'd always known he wasn't her first priority. "Enough dark talk. Back to our date. Dancing with you was amazing, and I'm ready for more."

Ready for the distraction from those thoughts from the past peppering him like buckshot.

"But it's still raining." She looked upward. The storm still hammered along the roof.

"There's space over by the fiddle player." He pointed toward the musician perched on a barstool. "We can make our own dance floor."

Smiling, she stood and tucked close against his side as he wove through the crowd, past staff and guests, toward the quaint corner. Music and rain, the perfect romantic ambiance. The Top Dog's reputed healing magic at work?

Regardless, he was done questioning his good luck.

"Attention, everyone..." A strained voice echoed through the sound system and a quick look over showed Jacob with a microphone. The ranch owner's expression was stark. Worried. "The weather station has issued a tornado warning. There's been a touchdown on Main Street in Moonlight Ridge."

Chapter Twelve

Charlotte was scared. Even huddled in the cellar beneath the barn with the rest of the guests. Even with Declan's strong arms wrapped around her.

She couldn't reach her brother. Cell phone reception was out due to the storm. The O'Briens had a shortwave radio on in the corner, and they were in touch with staff on walkie-talkies.

Overhead, dim light shone from the industrial bulbs in the root cellar, illuminating the neat rows of canned goods in the shelving system to their left. Charlotte squeezed her eyes shut, taking in both the musty cool air and Declan's musky aftershave, which calmed her nerves.

A few deep inhales later, she opened her eyes again, scanning the cinder block room where they'd been holed up for the past thirty minutes. Fifty guests were scattered in clusters around the concrete floors. Outside, the storm still raged, the sound of hail tapping the door leading out.

After herding the guests down the wooden stairway in a speedy file, Hollie had detailed tornado safety protocol as Jacob passed out water bottles from the shelves. If they grew hungry, she had snack packs they kept on hand for welcome baskets.

Declan's arm wrapped tighter around her and she buried her face in his chest, his heartbeat a dependable, soothing metronome. His fingers trailed protectively down her arm as the wind howled outside. "As far as cellars go to wait out a storm, this one isn't too shabby."

"It's a part of the Top Dog plan, always providing safe accommodations in any situation. Storing supplies in here serves a dual purpose in giving us plenty of water, food, blankets and lanterns." There was even a small bathroom in a far corner. Thank goodness. "I just wish I could talk to my brother."

Declan whispered softly into her ear, his gravelly voice warm. "Don't worry. I'm sure Rory is in the cellar under the stables with the staff over there."

"Then why can't Jacob reach him?" She rubbed her hands up and down her arms to ward off the chill that couldn't be totally attributed to the subterranean accommodations. Blinking back tears, she did her best to be calm, especially as she saw the scared faces of young children staring up at their parents.

"Any number of reasons." Declan snagged a small fleece blanket off the shelf behind them, a signature Top Dog piece with a paw-print-and-horseshoe pattern. He draped the fluffy throw over her shoulders. "Most likely, they've got their hands full with animals they took down with them—dogs, cats, sheep maybe, too."

"The horses must be freaked out." She chewed her bottom lip, leaning into Declan as an older couple inched by. "I don't even want to think about what would happen to them if the barn's damaged."

"No need to borrow trouble," he said reassuringly. "It's been my experience on the force that most of these warnings turn into nothing more than a few downed trees."

This probably wasn't the time to share the news that she, her brother and mom had once lived in a trailer park that had been decimated by a tornado. They'd lost everything and had to go on government assistance. Her mother had barely been able to get out of bed for two months. Charlotte had been sixteen then. Rory was two, and she'd done everything for him, even quit her job in the garden department at a local chain store. To earn money, she would babysit, since families usually let her take him along.

Family was important.

Her head on Declan's shoulder, she counted steady heartbeats, taking comfort in his warm strength, but in this frightening moment, she was still wary of trusting him for the long haul. Pockets of whispered conversations echoed around her. She could practically feel the collective unease in the cellar unfurling around her. "I imagine you'll be needed at work the minute the storm warning lifts."

"Afraid so." He skimmed his fingers along her jaw. "I'm sorry I'll have to cut our date short. I was having a great time with you. Maybe I could come by after? If it's not too late."

"Yes, please." She gripped the edges of the blanket, tugging it closer around her. "And don't worry about the time."

Angling back her head, she gave him a quick kiss, so thankful to have him with her. His smile warmed her all the way to her toes.

"Declan?" Jacob called from across the cellar. "Do you mind coming over here for a second? I'm trying to boost the signal on the walkie-talkies." He gestured to the different radios and devices on a wood table near the closed doorway.

"Sure," Declan said, standing and dusting off his jeans and smiling down at Charlotte. "I'll be right back."

She allowed herself the luxury of watching him, really watching him, taking in his lean frame that she knew carried whipcord strength. His wet hair was even darker, drawing her attention to his angularly handsome face, his strong jaw. Her body tingled at the thought of having him in her bed again.

A cleared throat startled her and Charlotte followed the sound to find Eliza standing on the other side of her, holding a box full of snack packets.

Kneeling, Eliza tipped the box toward her, showing an assortment of individually wrapped crackers, granola bars and trail mix. "Would you like something to eat?"

"I'm good, thank you." Was it possible her meal with Declan had only been twenty to thirty minutes ago?

"Do you mind if I sit with you for a minute?" she asked, hugging the box. "I could use a snack—and some company while I eat it."

Charlotte patted the space next to her that Declan had vacated. "Please, do. If you don't mind my saying, you look exhausted."

"I am, actually." Eliza set aside the box, snagged a blanket and set it on the floor like a cushion. "I worked all day, then played in the band this evening. It's been a long one."

"Any word from Doc Barnett?" Her friend had to be worried sick about her fiancé and his two grandkids. She was worried, too. The Top Dog Dude Ranch had a way of weaving people together into a family all its own.

"We were able to exchange a couple of texts before the lines overloaded from so many emergency calls." She toyed with her engagement ring, a glittering infinity twist. "He and the little ones are in the basement, under the stairway, having an impromptu tea party."

"You two make such a beautiful couple." Her gaze was drawn right back to Declan. Could the two of them piece together a relationship as strong? What was the magic formula?

"He's a great guy. Nolan made such a grand gesture in relocating here for me so I could keep my dream job at the ranch." She pressed the back of her hand to her forehead, sigh turning into a wide smile. "I guess everyone can see how much I adore that man."

"You're lucky to have found each other." Her chest went tight with anxiety over the future. It had been simpler to take one day at a time before the baby. But focusing on the here and now was worrisome enough. "I pray the greenhouse isn't affected by the storm. I have so much work for the festival stored there. So many plants I've nurtured from seedlings. How's everything over in the stable? Any word?"

"I'm stressing, big-time, but from the second that tornado warning came down, Jacob wouldn't let me leave here. He said the assistant manager could handle things at the stable with the staff on duty." Eliza sifted through the box of snacks and pulled out a package of trail mix, opening the package. All around them, the whispered conversations continued. "He pointed out that everyone was on lockdown, including himself, so as not to risk getting into a situation that required rescuing."

"That makes sense." The thought of Declan being in harm's way made her throat constrict. A trickle of unease went through her as she realized that worry for him wouldn't end once the storm passed. He was a cop. And their lives were tied together forever.

"On a positive note—" Eliza popped a cashew and raisin into her mouth "—at least the horses were already in their stalls for the night."

"I hope Rory's work there has been helpful." Thank goodness he and Rosie weren't alone. "I'm sure they were glad to have an extra set of hands in the stables tonight."

Eliza frowned. "What do you mean?"

"Rory told me he was working extra hours this evening to clear his debt sooner. I'm so glad he took Rosie with him. Otherwise, she'd have been in the house alone, probably terrified."

Eliza shifted to face her more fully. "Charlotte, honey. Rory's not at the stables. He left early this afternoon, looked really sick. I thought you knew. I left you a voice mail. Didn't you get it?"

Her heartbeat stumbled, fear and disappointment making her stomach sink.

Charlotte shook her head. All that anxiety, worry, fear that she'd worked so hard to tamp down gathered in a huge wad in her gut. "No, I didn't."

Because she'd been too wrapped up in her resurrected relationship with Declan.

"Oh, my." Eliza's eyes went wide with worry as she glanced toward the door, then back at Charlotte. "I am so sorry. So you don't know where he is?"

As if she wasn't already frightened out of her

mind. Now she had no idea where Rory could be in the middle of a catastrophic storm. It took an effort to pull herself together enough to force words from her dry throat, her tongue stuck to the roof of her mouth as fear paralyzed her.

"I haven't a clue," she admitted, tears stinging her eyes at the dangerous scenarios her mind was already conjuring.

As the storm raged outside, an equally strong force picked up speed inside her, whirling into full-blown panic for her little brother.

Sitting in the passenger side of Olivia's minivan with Rosie in his lap, Rory cursed the decision they'd made to keep driving in the bad weather. It hadn't seemed like a concern when they'd left, but later on, it had gotten genuinely scary. As the rain picked up, he'd worried about getting in a wreck—like Kai and Truitt had during a snowstorm. But Olivia was a really good driver.

Until they'd gotten the tornado warning alert on their cell phones and heard the sirens echoing through the mountains. As soon as they knew a tornado was coming, they'd pulled off the road into a gas station and took shelter in the men's room.

The grossest ninety minutes of his life. Thinking about it still made him gag.

While they'd hunched on the slightly sticky floor of the men's room, the only thing that had kept Rory calm was Rosie's gentle heartbeat. She'd curled in his arms, licking his hand, sharing her affection with him and Olivia both, as if the dog could sense how much they both needed her.

He'd been grateful to the dog for offering Olivia comfort that Rory would have been powerless to give on his own. Those ninety minutes were the longest of his whole life. They had given him so much time to think of everything that had gotten super messed up.

Once the threat of a tornado had passed, he washed his hands in scalding-hot tap water and got back on the road to go home. Olivia had been as eager to leave as him, practically sprinting back to the van to drive back to the ranch. If he didn't get there soon, Charlotte would realize he was missing. If she hadn't already.

Trees swayed overhead, showering leaves and pine straw along with the rain. Even a little hail. He didn't want to think about damage to Olivia's parents' minivan. There was already a tiny crack in the windshield.

And it had all been for nothing since the whole trip to see his mom had been a bust.

After he got to the facility, the nurse at the desk told him that the roommate was unavailable and his mother didn't want to see him. That she was in a very fragile state and it was for the best that they let her heal.

Not even the offer of Rosie could get him past the entrance.

His heart had fallen through the floor at the news.

There would be no answers to his question of why his mom did what she did. Or why he had to be the one to find her. Was she so mad at him she meant for him to be the one to see that?

Slumping down farther in his seat, he wished he could just disappear and magically transport to the cabin. He couldn't even bear the thought of Olivia's eyes full of sympathy. Pity.

Instead, on their drive back, he'd mostly fallen silent. Eyes fixed out on the road as he replayed the awful scene at the hospital again and again.

Muscle memory guided his hand as he scratched Rosie between the ears. She snoozed in his lap in a tight circle, snoring lightly.

Rory tightened one of the lopsided bows on Rosie's ears. "I don't want you to wreck or anything, but do you think you can go any faster?"

"If I get a ticket, my parents will know I took the car, then I'll never get to drive again until I graduate." Pale blue dashboard lights reflected onto Olivia's determined face as she carefully guided the SUV on the roads that continued to fill with water. Rain hadn't fully stopped even though the threat from the tornado had receded.

"Well, if we don't get home soon, they're gonna find out anyway."

"Zoey and Corrine are covering for us. I'm sure my friends won't rat me out. Besides," she said, pointing ahead, her hand bumping a tiny mooncatcher dangling from the rearview mirror, "we're almost there."

The Top Dog Dude Ranch welcome sign was just barely visible ahead through the dark and sheeting rain. The minivan jostled along, sloshing through the puddles of water.

"How can you be sure your friends won't say anything?" He didn't know who he could trust these days.

Olivia guided the minivan around a downed tree carefully. Once they were safely around the storm debris, she accelerated. "Zoey borrowed her folks' car a few days ago for her and Corrine to go out with Truitt and Kai."

"Oh man. I didn't know." There had been a time when he'd thought he and his buddies were tight. Now? They barely spoke.

"Yeah, well," Olivia continued as they passed the ranch's wooden placard, gravel crunching under the tires as they closed in on the sign, "Zoey let Truitt drive, and apparently...he did doughnuts in the pasture. She was really upset. So I promised her I wouldn't let you get behind the wheel."

Her words hit him in the gut. The silence stretched between them as they picked their way along the road toward his cabin. Only a few cars were out, and a handful of people walking with their umbrellas pushed into the wind.

"That was them?" He thought of all Charlotte's overtime covering the mess. "Because of them, my sister's been having to work overtime to fix the damage."

"Rory, come on," she said, all judgy sounding. Blinker on, she turned, avoiding more debris. On the wide turn, the mooncatcher swayed. "It was just a prank."

Really? How could she say that? "A prank is when you put sugar in the salt shaker. They damaged property, made a lot of trouble for people."

"You're one to talk." She shot him a pointed look. "Didn't you break into the gift shop and spray-paint all over the wall?"

Her words stung. And her cranky tone stung even more.

"I did, and it was wrong and stupid. The night almost wrecked my life." He stared over at her, confused at how clueless she sounded.

"Chill out," Olivia said, her voice rising with anger. Tearing her gaze from the road, she turned to look at him, her normally pretty face knotted with annoyance. "I thought you were fun. You sure didn't say no when I offered to borrow my parents' car without permission."

"You're right. And I'm sorry." He looked down at Rosie, so cute with the pink bows he'd carefully placed on her ears after brushing her. He let his hand drift in to the fur on her back, giving her a good scratch. Something sifted to the surface inside him. "I should have said no."

"What fun would that have been?" she asked sarcastically, not nice at all like she'd been before.

He nodded, not bothering to point out that this night hadn't been fun at all, between getting kicked out of his mom's facility and sitting on the floor in a smelly men's bathroom. His jeans still probably stank.

Olivia drummed her fingers on the steering wheel, her face all huffy. "Well, I guess it doesn't matter anyway since I'm leaving soon. This is as good a time as any to break it off."

That was it? Frustration cranked inside him. Along with a hefty dose of kicking himself. What had he been thinking? Of course she wasn't really interested in him. He'd been stupid to think she meant all that garbage about getting a summer job here. Truitt and Kai had moved on. Olivia was through with him.

His cell buzzed in his pocket with an incoming text, then again, repeating as a flood came through, startling Rosie with the unrelenting intensity. The pup hopped off his lap, onto the floorboards. He fished out his phone and found over a dozen texts from his sister, some older, like—there's a tornado warning and let me know you're ok. And others clearly newer like—call me now and get home ASAP.

Of all the ways today had gone sideways, this was the worst. Disappointing his sister. Again.

Because her messages made it clear that his cover about working in the stables was blown. There was no escaping it. He was busted.

* * *

As Rory pulled up in the minivan, Charlotte was so angry she was shaking inside as she sat on the top step, under the porch, the rain having slowed to a drizzle. She reminded herself that she needed to keep a cool head when talking to her brother. Seeing him climb out of the front seat, holding Rosie, relief warred with frustration.

At least he was alright. That was what mattered most.

Those minutes between when she'd heard about his latest stunt and when she'd finally been able to get a message through to him had felt like an eternity. Declan had been a steady support, already checking in with the station to see if any accident reports had come in matching Rory's description.

Once she'd heard from her brother, however, Declan had to leave for work, only pausing long enough to drop her off at her cabin on his way out. The tornado hadn't appeared to touch down at the ranch, but there wasn't word yet about the state of downtown Moonlight Ridge. Charlotte had to balance her worry for Rory with concerns for Declan, whose job could put him in danger in the storm's aftermath.

Now, she watched as Rory's blond hair fell in front of his eyes as he stared downward at the stone path. Even from here, she could tell her brother was in pain from the way his shoulders sagged. Rosie pranced next to him, avoiding the puddles gathering between the stones.

Once they were inside the picket fence, he unclipped Rosie's leash. "I guess I'm grounded and will be shoveling out stables until I graduate. Don't worry, though. I won't be going out again anyway. Olivia and I broke up."

She was too pummeled by her own emotions to make sense of his right now. He was upset, obviously. But had he been hurt? What had happened to him in those minutes when the sky had gone an unearthly dark green and static with the electricity of a deadly storm?

"I'm just glad to see you." She gripped the top step until her palms stung, trying to hang on to her tattered control. "You're not hurt? There was a tornado that touched down."

"I know. When we heard about it, Olivia and me stopped at a gas station to wait it out." He scrubbed his wrist under his nose. "We're not stupid."

She wanted to shout that this was absolutely a *stupid* stunt, but that would be counterproductive. And something in his face made her tread warily. He looked...wounded?

Seeing that he was unscathed physically at least gave her more emotional wherewithal to talk rationally to him.

Charlotte patted beside her on the step for him to sit. She hoped he would talk to her. "Where were you before the tornado warning?"

He dropped down beside her, Rosie's leash hanging from his tight fist. "Olivia drove me to visit Mom."

That revelation took the wind right out of her sails. She slumped back against the porch post. She wasn't quite sure what to do with that. "If you wanted to see her, you know I would have gone with you."

"I've gone with you before and Mom wouldn't let me in." His shoulders slumped and he retied his laces, his face hidden. "I thought maybe if I showed up alone with Rosie then maybe..."

"Did you see her?" she asked, hoping her gut was wrong even though everything about his dejected face told her otherwise. How many more times would their mother let him down?

"She wasn't feeling good." He shrugged, tossing aside the leash. "They said she's 'fragile.' They wouldn't even let her roommate see Rosie."

He'd taken the dog to see her previous owner? A tidal wave of emotion swept through her until tears welled.

"I'm sorry you made the trip for nothing." She blinked back tears, wanting to hug him but knowing he would pull away.

"No big deal." His chin tipped with false bravado. "Now I know she really doesn't want to see me. Sorry for thinking it was about you. That wasn't fair."

"None of this is fair." She searched for the right words to help him understand something she still struggled with herself. "You and I don't deserve what happened with Mom. But I do hope you can find some peace in knowing none of this is deliberate. She's doing the best she can."

"How come you're always able to do better?" He shot her a wary sideways glance.

That answer was simpler to address. Distant thunder rumbled. "Because I don't have mental health issues."

A light stream of water dripped down the copper rain chains hanging from the sides for the cabin, pinging off-kilter since they were tangled from the heavy wind. The wind chimes lay on the porch. Rory shut his eyes tightly, tension setting his mouth into a straight line.

"What if I do?" He seemed to shrink into himself, closing up with insecurity. Rory blanched, his words rasping. "I'm so mad all the time, Charlotte, it scares me."

A sigh wracked through her as she sifted through how best to answer him. The weight of finding the right words wasn't lost on her. Her brother didn't lower those walls often. "I would say you have reason to be angry. We both do, really. For what it's worth, when I'm with you, I don't see any of the signs of Mom's disease. And trust me, I've been looking—at you and at myself."

Rory's eyes were slightly glassy as he met her stare, a slow bob of the head. He seemed to be processing all she'd said. Clouds overhead gave way to bits of blue. A blue jay confidently sang and the thrum of crickets in the still-wet grass sounded.

Rory rubbed his palms hard along his jeans. "Thanks for not flipping out."

"Make no mistake, I'm totally flipping out on the inside," she said with a gentle smile.

He took a big breath. Something still had him concerned. The shadows on his face seemed to grow as he rubbed his arm. Looking downward, he kicked the ground with the tip of his sneaker. "Well, um, I should go ahead and tell you the rest."

Alarm bells went off inside her just when she was starting to catch her breath. "Okay, I'm listening."

"Olivia told me it was her friends Zoey and Corrine, with Truitt and Kai, who did the doughnuts out in the pasture." He held up a hand, his eyes meeting hers dead-on. No avoidance. "I swear it wasn't me and I didn't even know about it until tonight. But I can see why you might not believe me."

At least that was one mystery solved, and she was glad that her brother had been honest with her when he could have hidden this nugget of information. "I appreciate your telling me how it happened."

His forehead pinched with worry. "Are you gonna get in trouble at work because of me running off with a guest and what her friends did?"

Charlotte took heart that he finally realized on some level that his actions had consequences for others. "I'm sure it will be awkward for Hollie and Jacob if they decide to broach the subject with Zoey's and Corrine's parents. At least we know what happened."

"Okay, then," Rory said. "Is it alright if I go upstairs now? I really need a shower."

"Sure," she said, feeling pretty worn out herself. She wouldn't mind soaking in a bubble bath for an hour—or a week.

Rory angled over to hug her so fast she almost would have thought she imagined it.

Once the door slammed behind him, all the emotions of the night overwhelmed her, tears rolling down her face, sobs knocking at her ribs. She'd gone through a lot, but Rory had been going through even more, questioning his mental health even as his own mother rejected him over and over.

No wonder he'd been acting out. She didn't know how to help ease that pain for him, no matter how much she wished she could. Her life was as messed up as the broken wind chimes lying on the porch.

As she sat watching little Rosie get her paws muddy, Charlotte thought of all that had happened since the night her brother broke into the gift shop. What hurt most right now was that somehow, with one look at Declan, she'd allowed herself to lose sight of how emotionally wrecked her brother was.

She'd gotten so caught up in her own hurt over their breakup, allowing herself to worry about a future with their child that hadn't even happened yet when her brother's needs were 100 percent in the present moment. She'd seen how the distraction of being with Declan took her eyes off her brother during this critical time for him.

Rather than using the months of her pregnancy to explore some fling with Declan, she needed to have her focus firmly on getting her brother on the right path before she added a baby to the mix. So, she decided, she would handle this the way she'd done all her life. She would depend only on herself. She had to. Because too many others were depending on her.

Even though her heart screamed out in denial, she knew now that she would have to end the affair with Declan.

Chapter Thirteen

Declan threw his SUV in Park in front of Charlotte's cabin, just as the morning sun was peeking up. The vehicle was idling, but he was operating full steam ahead on adrenaline and caffeine.

Since he'd dropped Charlotte off last night, he'd checked into work, reviewed data on the tornado, dispatched officers throughout Moonlight Ridge and outlying areas. But so far, there was no major damage. Just a few fallen trees near the Christmas tree farm and two power lines down. The electric company was already on the site.

It appeared they'd dodged a bullet.

Now, he just wanted to sit down in Charlotte's kitchen and share a simple meal with her.

He ached for the everyday pleasures of sharing

a coffee and tea after a stress-filled night. He could prepare her favorite breakfast dish, huevos rancheros, and take satisfaction in making her morning a little easier. A mental image of Charlotte biting into the dish, flashing him a warm smile while her blond hair pooled over her shoulders, had him picking up his pace.

Swinging open the gate of the picket fence, he avoided some downed tree branches, which he would clear for her later in the day. Anything to help get this place back to normal.

Beneath his boots, still-damp steps groaned. He knocked on the door three times. There seemed to be no movement coming from the house. A strange quiet blanketed his wait before he heard the door unlock. Hinges that needed some WD-40 creaked open, warm yellow light filling the door frame.

Charlotte stood in the open doorway, her hair still damp from a shower, swept back with a headband. She was clearly dressed for work, wearing a Top Dog T-shirt and loose overalls rolled up at the ankles. She scrunched her toes, her favorite Crocs resting by the front door.

She was so beautiful his teeth ached.

He rubbed a tight spot along his rib cage. "Do you mind if I come in?"

Charlotte stepped out onto the porch and closed the door behind her. Clouds turned her light blue eyes stormy as she folded her arms across her chest, face tight. "Do you mind if we sit out here? Rory's still sleeping. I don't want him to wake up and overhear us talking."

A twinge of unease crept up his spine, but he tamped it down. "Sure, it'll be good to take a load off my feet for a minute."

She gestured to the porch swing and he took a seat. Adjusting his weight to keep the swing still, he made room for her to sit on the pink cushion next to him. Except she didn't join him. Instead, she leaned against the porch post, her arms crossed over her chest, her baby bump just barely visible. "Any news on damage?"

"Nothing major, thank heavens." He kept his eyes lasered in on her, trying to gauge her mood. Maybe she was just tired. "It skirted the edges of the Christmas tree farm, then lifted up again as if hopping over the ranch. By the time it touched down again near the Sulis Springs cave, the storm had fizzled out."

"That's good news."

Her curt expression did little to alleviate his unease. She looked beyond him, and he swiveled his head to see what had caught her eye. His gaze caught on Charlotte's carefully maintained beautiful planters, filled with a rainbow of delicate flowers. Yesterday's storm had upturned the planters pressed against the fence, and now large branches were crushing her tender flowers. Was that what was upsetting her? No, it couldn't be, she was barely looking at them. It seemed she was simply staring off into space.

"I'll still need to check out more of the town, but it seems we got off easy." Declan faced front again, back to Charlotte. "Did you get everything straightened out with Rory?"

She nodded, her gaze skirting away as she leaned to straighten a fallen potted plant, then brushed the dirt off the porch with her fingers. "He'd snuck off to see our mother, but she wasn't up for a visit."

Ah. Now her reserved mood made more sense. Part of the tension he carried deep in his chest rushed from him with a deep sigh.

He rubbed the back of his neck. "I'm sorry about that."

"You have nothing to be sorry about." Straightening, she dusted her hands along her pants legs. "But I should let you know it appears that Kai and Truitt were the ones who tore up the pasture. They went joy riding with some girls visiting here. They used a car belonging to one of the girls' parents."

"Whoa, okay." Not a surprising outcome as it had reeked of a teenage prank. He was just glad Rory hadn't been involved. "Thanks for letting me know. I'll take it from here. But I'll come back after the morning shift. We can have lunch together. Maybe even snag a catnap."

She backed up a step, with a dismissive wave. "No need to worry about me. You're probably ready for your own bed."

"I want to spend time with you. Our date was cut short earlier," he stated, trying to be clear and calm. "I'm not asking to spend the night. We could sit on the porch, watch the sunset."

"Look," she said, straightening, "I'm drained and don't want to talk today."

The last thing he wanted was to wear her out, especially at a time when she needed her rest more than ever. Still, he sensed something else was at play with her. "What's really going on here?"

"Not now." Her voice was soft, and she held up a hand as if needing to keep distance between them. "This isn't the right time."

"I think it's exactly the right time." He was done ignoring the warning bells inside him. He didn't want to let unhappy feelings fester. Sweat popped along the back of his neck as the uncertainty nagged at him. Facing any bad news would be better than waiting with this dread.

"If you must know, right now—" she stressed the last two words, blue eyes more serious than he'd ever seen them "—I appreciate all you've done to help things run smoother between us and I enjoyed the night we spent together."

Nothing she said sounded bad, per se, but the tone had him worried. Morning birds chirped, flitting through the yard. Their cheery song ill fitting this moment and the somber look on her face.

"Charlotte, let me stop you there—"

"No," she cut him off, voice definitive. "We've started this conversation, so I'm going to see it through. I've come to the conclusion that you were correct when you broke things off between us—"

"*You* were the one to ask for a break," he interjected gently.

"A break. Just a break. Then you leaped at the chance to end things completely. And now things are even more complicated with Rory and the baby. You and I have so much baggage from growing up. I don't want to risk giving that same kind of legacy to Rory and our child."

Even though he'd sensed the rejection was coming, her words gut-punched him. He rubbed his thumb atop the smooth wood of the porch swing, needing to figure out how to navigate from here. "What are you talking about? Haven't we moved past that breakup?" He searched for an angle to de-escalate the conversation. "I'm not pressuring you. I thought we agreed to simple dates."

"I hoped we could do that, but I can't help but think you have an agenda here." She bent over to pick up another piece of storm debris, a small branch, and tossed it into the yard.

He understood her agitated energy all too well. He was feeling plenty of it himself, but if he wanted to reassure her after the stress of the last twelve hours, he needed to remain composed.

"Fine, I'll admit it. I want us to move in together," he said, calibrating his voice to stay soothing. Calm. Hopefully persuasive.

But already she was shaking her head. "We've been over this..."

Standing, he continued, determined, "I want to revisit the subject."

Her hand gravitated to his chest and rested softly over his heart. For a moment he took hope.

She breathed in deeply in the way she often did before kissing him. His heart worked overtime, his fingers twitching as he began to raise his hand to clasp hers.

"Declan, I'm sorry," she said gently, dashing any optimism. "I promise you can be a part of our child's life, but you and I are never going to be a couple. I was fooling myself that we could simply date—coast along doing whatever feels good—when so much is at stake. With the baby on the way, I need to focus on my family."

The implication was all too clear. He wasn't a part of her family circle, even with the baby, and that stung. "That's exactly why I want to be involved. Because I want a role in our child's life and, if nothing else, that makes us both part of the family to this child."

Already, she was shaking her head. "You've never worked past the problems that made you break up with me—and break my heart—in the first time. I can't risk that kind of ending to a relationship again."

"Things are different now, with the baby," he pressed, sensing any chance with her was fast slipping from his grasp.

"Which is the precise reason why I can't afford to mess this up, Declan, and neither can you." Her eyes sheened with tears, but she blinked them away quickly. "Once the May Day festival is over, I want us to see an attorney about drawing up a formal custody agreement."

Her hand fell away, and while he stood there stunned still, she pivoted quietly on her heels, disappearing through the front door. Closing it behind her. Firm. Clicking in place a barrier between them.

As he sagged back against the porch railing, all the adrenaline left his body, leaving nothing but the exhaustion of the night. More than just the night. Weariness from decades. Could she be right that their baggage left him too damaged, incapable of a stable future? Maybe she hadn't said that exactly, but it was what he heard, what he felt all the way to his aching bones as he lumbered down the stairs.

He'd been through so many tense situations, dangerous circumstances. But he couldn't recall a time where he felt the thrum of his heart so acutely.

With each step out of her white-picket-fence world, he kept replaying their previous breakup in his head, every word reinforcing that here they were again…over…

Declan stretched his feet in front of him, the terracotta chiminea on Charlotte's patio radiating heat into the early evening. And somehow it didn't chase away the chill in his gut over what he had to tell Charlotte. It didn't help that she was looking far too appealing in her bright pink parka and blond braids, a natural beauty.

Their relationship was still so new, he didn't know how she would react. Especially since she'd been acting so distant and distracted from the moment Rory's text had come in during their night at the springs. He wanted to believe her new reserve was a product of his imagination, but he'd been a cop too long to ignore his instincts.

"Thank you for coming over." Charlotte leaned forward in her chair, holding her gloved hands closer to the fire, her every gesture twitchy and nervous as they sat outside her two-bedroom cabin. "I don't want to risk leaving Rory alone, not after his last stunt."

"I'm just glad he's okay." Declan had seen too much—done too much in his own youth—not to be concerned for the boy. Which meant he worried about Charlotte as well and the challenges she faced in handling a troubled teen.

"I appreciate your understanding." Her blue eyes filled with gratitude that almost pushed away a deep sadness lurking. A kindling stick in hand, she swirled the melting snow around the chiminea. "I need you to know I really enjoyed our time together in the cave and I don't regret making love with you, not for a moment..."

He went stone-still, all his instincts cranking on high alert again, telling him something bad was coming. "But?"

"But I think we should take a break," she said

quickly, wrapping her arms around herself, her hands rubbing along her sleeves. "The timing of this is all wrong with my brother moving here. He's not a bad kid, there's just so much baggage with our parents that he needs to deal with... I have to focus all my attention on making sure he's on the right path."

She eyed him warily, silently waiting for his response as she leaned forward in her Adirondack chair.

Frustration seared through him, because being with Charlotte had been incredible, and not just because of the sex. She was a funny, smart woman. In fact, she was so smart that he knew she was right.

Rory needed her.

Declan's eyes flicked to her log cabin and the warm glow of the lights pouring out the window. He could make out Rory's head in the shadows, angled toward the TV.

The kid was a ticking time bomb and the window of time to defuse him was short. Knowing and accepting that made it simpler for him to tell her... "I, uh, got some news today. I'm being called up, National Guard duty."

Her forehead furrowed. "Your regular weekend training?"

Drumming his fingers on the arm of his chair, he stared hard at the melting snow. The heat of the chiminea decimated the surrounding snow, leaving a mess.

"No. Longer than that. I'm being activated."

Standing, she circled over to him, sitting on the edge of the chair. "Where? For how long?"

The worry stamped all over her face only amplified his resolve that he needed to let her go. He couldn't add more burdens to her already overloaded life.

Declan surveyed the grounds, trying to soak in all the details of this place—the spilt rail fence, the perfectly decorated garden, the amazing woman right in front of him. "The details haven't been confirmed yet, although I know it will be soon. It feels like a sign, given what you just said." Rising, he took her hands in his and pulled her up with him. "I've enjoyed our time together these past couple of weeks. You're an incredible lady, but it's over."

"Wait," she said, squeezing his fingers, her cheeks rosy from the wind, as pink as her parka. "I know what I said earlier, but... If you have an address, I'll write."

He appreciated her big heart, the way she couldn't let him leave for military duty with a fresh breakup.

It said a lot about her.

And maybe that was just one more reason why he needed to accept that they couldn't be together.

"No," he said firmly, telling himself it was for the best. "We've had a fling and it's over. I'm not a white-picket-fence kind of guy. This is goodbye."

Since the tornado and breaking things off with Declan three days ago, Charlotte had worked from sunup to sundown to avoid thinking or feeling. Or hurting. She wasn't having much success with that last one. With each day that passed, she missed him all the more.

She'd read on one of her favorite blogs that it would get easier. But it hadn't, not for a moment. If she were being honest, she'd been hurting since the day he had been activated for Guard duty and shattered her world.

And after tomorrow's May Day festival, future dealings between them would be based on nothing more than a legal document. The thought made tears sting her eyes. Prescriptive meetings. Her mind whirred to all of the heartache she hadn't yet experienced. Having a child together meant she would watch Declan move on in real time. There would be no hiding from that fact, the evolution.

She blinked the tears away and focused on helping Gwen stock the shop shelves. The May Day event would be open to the public. Gwen had stayed at the greenhouse until her boys' bedtime yesterday to help her get everything ready, and this was Charlotte's chance to return the favor.

Their friendship was a gift. And if ever she'd needed a friend, now was the time.

Charlotte gathered a small stack of blue boxes in her arms, making her way to the oak shelf. The scent of lemongrass lingered in the air, concentrated by the shelf. A few weeks ago, she'd experimented infusing herb oils into cleaning products. Gwen had enthusiastically agreed to test out her new formula. At least she had gotten the chemistry right on something these past few weeks.

Exhaling, she placed the blue jewelry boxes on the shelf, careful to separate gold necklaces with dog charms from the silver. The gift shop was more than some kitschy tourist trap. Gwen had created a place with tasteful items at all price points.

Charlotte's fingers lingered over a silver-horse charm bracelet. The sparkly pink one she selected shone bright in the store's soft overhead lighting. Pink for a baby girl? "I know it won't be easy, but I'll manage like other single moms."

"What about Declan?" Gwen asked, tightening the tie on her work apron.

She followed Gwen into the stockroom. Her friend pointed to the containers of pickled red peppers that had been grown on the ranch. Grabbing a nearby green basket, Charlotte loaded several jars as they made their way back to the front of the store. "Declan says he wants to be involved with the baby. He's even pushing for us to move in together out of a misguided sense of duty. His mother struggled as single mom, and he doesn't want history to repeat itself. We're going to have a lawyer draw up a custody agreement after the May Day festival."

"That's not a bad thing, wanting to be a part of his child's upbringing," Gwen said gently, resting her hand on her necklace with her triplets' initials.

"I know, I truly do." Charlotte arranged the pickled red peppers next to the raspberry and strawberry jams. They were bestsellers in Gwen's store, the fresh fruit from the ranch canned using one of Hollie's family recipes. An involuntary ache squeezed in her chest at the family she had almost had with Declan, and for the first time considered what she would be naming her child.

Would she and Declan even be on speaking terms to discuss the choices? "I just can't subject Rory and the baby to the roller coaster of me being in an on-again, off-again relationship with Declan. It's too risky."

"Too risky for them?" Gwen eyed her knowingly while stylizing crystal jewelry made from Sulis Springs cave on a display wrapped with moss and dried flowers. "Or too risky for you?"

"All of the above?" she admitted to her friend and to herself as well.

Gwen placed a gorgeous crystal necklace, a pretty piece with a floral theme, then rested a hand on Charlotte's shoulder. "I understand that you want to protect your brother and the child you're carrying."

Charlotte straightened, surprised at the insinuation. "Are you telling me I'm the problem here?"

"I'm just saying that you have a right to be wary."

She made quick work of the display, then walked back to the storeroom. Charlotte followed with a furrowed brow, weaving past the corner of the store devoted to clothing. Her friend handed her a few paw print cookie jars.

They returned to the storefront and Charlotte placed the cookie jars on a shelf, turning over her friend's words.

Holding a few cowboy hats, Gwen arranged them on a wall next to the belt buckles and T-shirts.

Gwen continued speaking gently as she refastened the buttons on a shirt, straightening it on the hanger. "You've been through a lot with your mom, and the breakup with Declan. I can see why you wouldn't want to take that risk again."

Wary for herself?

Maybe Gwen was right. But if so, how was she supposed to get past the fear? She folded the open box of earth-toned onesies that featured scenes of puppies and children playing. Her heart squeezed so hard her breath was knocked from her.

The sound of the shop bell interrupted her thoughts.

Gwen raised a hand. "Hold that thought. I'll be right back."

On the table in the back of the store was a box of goods Charlotte had crafted. Handwoven flower crowns, wands and garland. Satchels of flower petals and herbs. Wreaths with spring flowers. Every item she'd poured her heart and soul into, all specially made for the festival. She picked up a few flower crowns and followed.

Her friend approached an older woman in a sapphire-blue dress with well-appointed silver jewelry that sparkled in the store's light. She was tall, regal even, with her steel gray hair twisted into a thick bun.

Gwen smiled. “Hello, Mrs. Greer. What brings you over this way today?”

The older lady trailed her fingers along the shelves of vintage toys, pausing on a hand-carved wooden block set. “I was out walking and got all turned around. I left my cell phone at home.” Confusion and worry clouded her eyes. “Would you be a dear and call my son?”

“Of course, happy to help.” She ducked behind the counter, angling by Charlotte as she placed a basket of May Day hair wreaths by the register.

Charlotte glanced over her shoulder, then back to Gwen. Quietly, she leaned over the counter. “Mrs. Greer? Any relation to the Christmas tree farmer Ian Greer?”

“Yes, she is his mother,” Gwen whispered. “Mrs. Greer has memory issues. She’s wandered in here at least once a week since she moved from her daughter’s home to live with her son.”

Charlotte had understood well what it was like to worry for a parent. Now, she also grasped the weight of worrying *as* a parent.

And even though her heart was breaking, she had to keep her child in mind and push ahead, a step at a time.

However, one thing was certain. Those steps had been easier when Declan was far away. Because she didn’t know how she would get through that meeting at the lawyer's office with Declan's handsome face across the table and the knowledge that she'd have to walk away and not look back.

Chapter Fourteen

Declan wished he hadn't volunteered to run security for the May Day festival. But when he'd agreed, he'd been trying to win back Charlotte, grasping at any opportunity to be with her. He'd never imagined things between them would end like this.

The ranch was humming with activity, packed by lunchtime. Was it any wonder he couldn't find Charlotte? And he'd looked. Hard. He didn't have a clue what he would say to her, but he did know that each night without her felt lonelier, the days hollower.

So he searched, the ranch a flood of color—shades of emerald green, pastel pink and sapphire blue. The ten-foot-tall Maypole was already in place in the center of a field, with Raise the Woof playing folk tunes nearby. Children ran and squealed, with flower crowns in their hair, lemon yellow ribbons streaming behind them. Others wore delicate fairy wings, all with floral touches that spoke of Charlotte's influence.

And the landscaping was magnificent. His work boots covered more ground as he searched the party for Charlotte. Although he had yet to spot her in person, he was seeing her everywhere in the stunning mix of vibrant wildflowers creating a palette of color. It was a display of pure artistry beyond anything he'd seen before. He wished he knew the names of each of them, that he'd paid more attention to Charlotte talking about her work.

Now, he could just take in the spectacle. The ranch's stone bonfire pit crackled off to the side, flames licking up to the sky. Hollie, wearing a peasant dress in the O'Brien tartan, divvied up bags of kettle corn cooked over the flames. Other partiers gathered round, cooking sausages and s'mores.

"Hey there, Sheriff," Doc Barnett's voice carried over the chaos.

Declan pivoted to find, just past a food truck, Doc Barnett was walking his fiancée's border collie, Loki. Micah Fuller, the ranch's contractor, kept pace with his mountain dog puppy, Jupiter. Both dogs sported collars decorated with dried flowers.

Micah adjusted his grip on the leash. "Where's your costume?"

Declan shrugged, looking down at his clean pressed pants and shined shoes. "I'm in uniform."

Micah took a sip of his lemonade, eyes following after his nephew, whose face was elaborately painted to resemble a lion. "Will we see you at the staff after-party?"

Doc Barnett adjusted the daisy in his shirt pocket. "The O'Briens even arranged for a catering company and hired a band so none of the staff would have to work the event."

Micah motioned to the kids singing as they looped around the Maypole, different-colored ribbons in each of their small hands. "I really enjoy how this community has such a family feel. I couldn't have chosen a better place to bring up Benji."

"Agreed." Doc Barnett looped his thumbs into his jeans pockets. He stepped back as a child dressed as a fairy princess bolted to a Top Dog staff member who played tunes on a tin whistle. "You and Charlotte—Rory and the baby, too—are a part of that family now."

Declan drew in a heavy sigh. Might as well get it over with since everyone would hear soon enough. "Charlotte and I broke things off. We're seeing an attorney tomorrow to draw up a custody arrangement for the baby."

Doc Barnett stopped, turning to speak, "Man, I am so sorry."

Micah halted in his tracks, Jupiter taking advantage of the opportunity to sniff a cluster of purple flowers. "That's rough."

"Yeah. She dumped me," Declan admitted. "She

says we have too much baggage from the past—like her mom and my mom."

Micah adjusted his grip on Jupiter's leash. "Where's your mother now?"

"She lives in California. She headed out that way with a boyfriend ten years ago. They broke up. She stayed. I offered to relocate her here, but she says she's happy with her friends."

"Well—" Micah clapped him on the shoulder "—you're a good son."

"I don't know about that." Declan waved off the praise, shoulders slumping, his gaze still searching for a glimpse of Charlotte. "We've had our rough patches, but she's my mom. I love her."

There had been a time he wouldn't have said that, back in his teenage years when he'd been full of rage. Like the time he'd saved all of his income from his after-school job bagging groceries, planning to buy a bike. His mom had gone away for an overnight with friends. He'd tripped over the dog and broke his ankle. He hadn't been able to reach his mother, so he'd gotten a neighbor to drive him to the hospital.

Child services had been alerted. His mom had decided it was best to have them step in this time as she worried about being able to pay the medical bill from his injury. He'd lost his job, had to move to another school. He'd chewed his mother out over that one, full of teenage anger at how little control he had over his life.

Why was he thinking about that now?

Micah clicked his tongue and Jupiter bounded toward him, eager for the treat he wrested from his pocket. “We’ve all got baggage. My brother had such a bad drug problem he chose that over his child. Then our parents wouldn’t even step up to take care of their grandchild.”

Declan pulled his mind from the past. “That’s awful.”

“Susanna has helped restore my faith in people.” Micah looked over to his fiancée wearing fairy wings and a poofy tulle dress as she gathered the children for their play about the legend of Sulis Springs.

Doc Barnett looked away as his grandchildren called out for him. He waved back then said, “We should head over that way if we want to get a good seat near the front. The Sulis Springs children’s play is fast becoming a staple in all major Top Dog events.” He turned to Declan. “Are you coming?”

Declan shook his head. “I’ll join you in a little bit.”

He needed a few minutes to get his head together.

Declan sighed deep, a mix of rose and lilac flooding his senses as he maneuvered past a cart selling flower crowns where young children and their families gathered. Distracted, he dropped onto a vacant wooden bench, the festival playing out around him.

He thought back to the broken-ankle memory and all that rage at his mom and life. He’d said he loved his mother, and that was true. But there were so many times when that feeling hurt worse than any broken ankle.

Everything went still inside him. Was that why he'd flinched so hard from any relationship? Why he'd taken the first opportunity to run from Charlotte? That moment when she'd asked for a break, it had been like the past repeating itself. Life spinning out of control. Losing a loved one.

A loved one?

The words settled deep inside him, sifting through all the years of anger, anger that had been masking pain. Now, his love for Charlotte swelled through him, pushing aside the hurt, bringing peace and balance to his soul.

He'd been letting baggage steal his future. But no longer.

Pushing to his feet, he scanned the crowd, searching for the love of his life. All around him, he saw everything his heart had always yearned for—togetherness and love, beauty and joy. He saw it in the way children reverently touched the flower creations, and felt it in the slow, melodic hum of the fiddle. While he couldn't find her, he did see someone who might have insights for winning Charlotte back, a person whom he already embraced as a part of the family he'd never expected to have.

"Hey, Rory," he called out to the teen walking Rosie through the sniff garden. "I need your help."

The day had come together beyond her expectations.

Carrying a basket of sachets, Charlotte threaded

through the crowd, passing out the packets of dried flowers. She'd woven blooms through her hair, wearing a peasant dress and apron, the ties emphasizing the growing curve of her stomach.

Fitting, given May Day was a celebration of fertility, birth and regrowth.

Children danced around the Maypole with long silk banners. Their flower wreaths streamed ribbons behind them.

Early today, the energy of the children flooded the scene around the Maypole. As the afternoon sun waned, the energy of the once-excited children also dwindled.

Exhaustion tugged at her but she knew it was more heart weariness than physical exhaustion. Though there was plenty of physical exhaustion, too. Sleep had been hard to come by since she'd cried her eyes out until three in the morning.

She forced a smile and passed the last sachet to Mrs. Greer, who was walking the festival on her son's arm. Turning away, Charlotte started the walk toward her cabin, grateful that the O'Briens had hired outside workers to clear up any mess so the staff could attend a catered party. Not that she was in a party mood.

At the end of the path where a section of violets bloomed, she opened the picket fence to her cabin. Rory waited on the front steps as Rosie toddled around the yard.

The teen still wore his Top Dog T-shirt he'd donned

to help in the stables during the festival, finishing up the last of his community service. "Hello, sissy. How are you doing?"

Her steps faltered. He hadn't called her *sissy* since moving in with her. She closed the gate and petted Rosie. "I'm tired, but I'll be okay."

She hoped if she said it often enough it might become true.

Rory scooted on the step to make room for her next to the big pot of wild ginger that had magically been spared by the storm. "I did the dishes."

"Thank you," she said, surprised. Heartened. She dropped to sit next to him. "I spoke with Mom's doctor today and he's going to help guide us through a meeting with Mom."

She'd called this morning, needing to make something positive happen. No more burying her head in the sand and hoping things would get better. Her brother was drowning trying to process their mother's mental illness. Charlotte had to admit it overwhelmed her, too, and she needed to get a grip on the situation before the baby was born.

The clinic counselor had given her information on their family group therapy program. The prospect gave her hope on one front at least, even if she'd lost the chance at a relationship with Declan.

Frowning, Rory cast her a sideways look. "What do you mean 'guide us'?"

"We won't be showing up unannounced." She detailed what she'd been told, praying he would be receptive. Heaven knew, it made her nervous to consider going. "It'll be part of a planned therapy session to meet with Mom and talk through what happened when she tried to hurt herself. The counselor will be present to help keep things from blowing up. What do you think?"

Rory brushed his hands along his khakis, his forehead furrowed in thought. Rosie scampered up the steps and settled in his lap. His hand moved to the pup, stroking. "I'd like that—if it's something you want, too."

She breathed a sigh of relief. At least something was going right in her life. "I would. Very much. And we're even going to be able to take Rosie into the session with us. After that, we can meet with Rosie's former owner out in the garden."

Straightening, he blinked fast, scrubbed his wrist over his eyes and lunged over to wrap her in a hug. "Thanks, Charlotte. Love you."

As soon as the hug began, it ended, so quickly she could almost think she'd imagined it. But she hadn't. "I love you, too, Rory."

She smoothed back the wayward lock of blond hair that fell across his brow. Quickly, though, before he could pull away or get defensive.

But he just grinned, standing and brushing his hands along his khaki shorts. "Oh, hey, about the reason I was waiting for you. There's some kind of emergency over at the Sulis Springs cave. You're needed right away."

"Alright," she said. Her nap would have to wait. "Who should I call?"

"You're supposed to come straight over," he insisted, putting the leash on Rosie. "Uh, everyone is too busy to answer the phone. I'll go with you. Just to make sure you get there okay."

Arguing with Rory would only disrupt the best conversation she'd had with him in months, maybe longer. So she stood, joining him as he led the way, holding Rosie's leash. The final echoes of the festival whispered through the trees as she made her way along the path, bordered by flowers and bushes in a natural way that mirrored the chaos of nature.

Paw print signs on trees pointed toward the Sulis Springs cave, but she knew the way. Memories of her date with Declan teased through her, brushing against her tender heart.

Picking her way through a clearing, she was careful to avoid the fire azaleas. After stepping onto the crisp, green grass, she paused, her heart leaping to her throat. The sight before her eyes feeling impossible, a mirage of May Day, induced with magical contact from fairy folk.

Declan?

He stole her breath, more so than anything else about this day.

As she took in the sight of him, so handsome in his uniform, a tidal wave of love hit her so hard she stumbled back a step. How could she have missed it for so long? She'd been lying to herself, thinking she was protecting her heart. But there was no denying the feeling pumping through her right now. She was in love with Declan.

A hint of panic twinged through her and she looked back for her brother. Except he was nowhere to be seen. Realization hit. She'd been set up.

For what reason?

"Declan, what's going on?" She'd been nervous enough about tomorrow's meeting with the lawyer.

"I needed to talk to you, somewhere we won't be interrupted." He gestured to the mouth of the cave. "This was the most private place I could think of today."

She rocked from foot to foot, still shaken by the realization of her feelings for Declan. "We have the appointment in the morning."

"Please?" He extended a hand.

Swallowing, she nodded, taking his hand and following him inside. She padded her way to the smooth gray stone walls surrounding the hot springs, filling the space with steam and memories.

Her heart hammered, rising into her throat as he led them to a carved bench. He motioned for her to sit on the sculpted stone, and she lowered herself down, almost afraid to breathe. He joined her, dropping the contact in a way that left her aching.

"Thank you," he said, his hands clasped between his knees. "I know that you have concerns, worries even. Big ones. And so do I. I don't want you to think

I'm making light of that in any way. But I need for you to understand I'm not going anywhere."

While a part of her wanted to be hopeful at those words, still she was wary. "Declan—"

"Hear me out." He rested a broad hand on her knee, squeezing gently. "I need to start by saying I'm so very sorry for the way I broke things off when I left for Guard duty. I think I was so afraid of getting too close to you for fear you would see the real me—the messed-up teen I'd once been."

She couldn't stop thoughts of him growing up, constantly let down by his mother, feeling rejected over and over. Was it any wonder he flinched from commitment?

"Apology accepted." She wished she could enjoy this moment with him, but she was still hurting from their break. Still aching inside from losing him, and that ache hurt all the more now that she realized she loved him. Steeling herself to leave, she said, "Thank you. But I should get back. It's almost time for the after-party."

Not that she felt much like celebrating.

"Hold on, please." He clapped his palm to his chest, over his heart. "Hear me out for a few more minutes, and then if you want to leave, I won't stop you."

Cool air lingered in the cave, giving her much-needed relief and clarity. Her eyes scanned the art along the stone walls, painted by the most recent guests. Washes of colors and hearts filled her vision, prompting her own heart to expand.

What more did she have to lose? She nodded for him to continue.

"I've been doing a lot of thinking over the past few days," he said, his deep voice rumbling through the cavern. "You and I have both faced some hefty challenges, and we haven't just faced them, we've overcome them. We are two people who learn from the past as we move forward. I believe we can do that as a couple."

Something stirred inside her.

"I'm listening." She waved for him to continue, more than intrigued. She hadn't heard this introspective side of him before.

"It's understandable that you don't trust me, trust that I can be here for you for the long haul." His voice cracked. "You'd asked me for space before, a break. It was a fair request and I answered that request by cutting you off. I need you to know that I panicked at the first sign of trouble, because you mean so much more to me than anyone I've ever met before."

Hope curled through her like the tendrils rising from the springs. Still, she needed to be cautious. "I think we both were afraid."

His head dipped for a moment before he continued, "All that has happened to us has made us stronger. So much so, that our first line of defense is independence." His gaze met hers, his brown eyes full of vulnerability, a deep openness he'd never shown before. "I've realized that isn't the best way after all."

Her heart beat faster. "What would the best way be? In your opinion?"

"Together," he said, clasping both her hands in his. "Sharing life's joys and burdens, stronger because we're together. And not just because of the baby. Not just because Rory needs guidance. But because I need you."

His words picked up speed and intensity. "I love you, Charlotte, with all my heart. I want to spend my life with you. As your husband."

The hope inside her blossomed, spreading joy and the perfume of anticipation to every part of her. "Are you finished?"

"Yes." He nodded quickly, his grip on her hands tightening as if he couldn't bear to let her go.

She understood the feeling well.

"Good, because I love you, too." Charlotte savored the feel of the beautiful words on her tongue. "I love your strength, your honor, your humor and thoughtfulness."

She slid her hands up to touch his dear face, a face that she looked forward to seeing change over the years. "I just love *you*, and more than anything, I want to be your wife."

A sigh wracked through him and she saw the depth of his worry that her answer might be different. She sealed her words, her vow, with a kiss, sinking into the sensation of being in his arms again. Now and forever.

Smiling, he eased back, smoothing a hand along her hair and releasing petals to float at their feet like a wedding trail. "There was a reason I arranged for you to meet me here. This place is where we had the best day of my life…until now. I have a gift to commemorate the start of our life together."

"A gift?" How had he arranged for that so quickly?

He reached under the bench and withdrew a small flat box with a bow, one she recognized from the gift shop. How sweet of him, so thoughtful. She could see his heart in his eyes. She tugged the satin ribbon and creaked open the jewelry box to find… She gasped.

A stunning silver-and-crystal necklace, one she'd arranged in the shop with Gwen just yesterday.

"It's so beautiful." She stroked her fingers along the crystal beads that glistened with light echoing the sparks inside her. "And made from crystals here in the cave."

His grin kicked a dimple into his bristly cheek. "I thought it fit with coming here." He pulled it from the box, holding it up for her. "I have to confess, I had a little help from Rory and Gwen."

She lifted her hair as he secured it around her neck, the jewels cool against her skin. Her delicate fingers felt the intricate flower-and-vine pattern as joy infused her breath.

"Thank you." She touched the necklace, hoping he could see the pleasure in her eyes. "It's perfect."

"I'm glad you like it." He set aside the box and took her left hand in his, stroking his thumb along her ring finger. “We can go ring shopping together so you can choose just what you want.”

“That sounds perfect.” How fitting that they should find their love for each other on this May Day celebration, a time of rebirth. She'd been gifted with this second chance, the birth of her future with Declan.

Rising, he tugged her hand. “Let's go celebrate with our friends—our family—at the after-party.”

“What a lovely way to announce our news,” she said, rising to slide her arms around him again. “But first, I want you to kiss the bride.”

Without hesitation, he did just that.

* * * * *

SPECIAL EXCERPT FROM

HARLEQUIN® SPECIAL EDITION

Sensible ER nurse Maggie Malone would never normally fall for handsome rancher Cordell Hollister. Maybe her best friend's wedding softened Maggie's stance on bad boys. Still, hundreds of miles separated Maggie's and Cordell's lives. There was no reason they'd ever see each other again. One positive pregnancy test later, however, and Cordell was offering Maggie a marriage of convenience. But would accepting for the baby's sake mean denying her feelings...or finally embracing them?

Read on for a sneak preview of
For the Rancher's Baby *by* USA TODAY
bestselling author Stella Bagwell.

Chapter One

Cordell Hollister never shied away from a party. Especially when the merrymaking included dancing, drinking and pretty girls. But tonight's event was more than a get-together of neighboring ranchers in need of a break before a hard Utah winter arrived. This was a wedding reception for his brother and sister-in-law, Jack and Vanessa. And anything to do with a wedding made Cordell uncomfortable.

For damned good reason. Being reminded of a time four years ago when he'd come close to getting married sent a cold chill down his spine. He'd shocked his fiancé, Lacey, and everyone in Beaver County, including his family, when he'd called off the whole shebang. But Cordell had only felt immense relief.

Now as he stood at the edge of the crowd, watching his friends and relatives dancing and laughing and sipping champagne, he was happy for Jack and his new wife. And even happier that *he* was still free and single.

Draining the last of his beer, he tossed the bottle in a nearby trash bin and was making his way through the crowd, when he felt a light tap on his back.

"Excuse me, Cord. I want you to say hello to someone."

His new sister-in-law Vanessa's voice managed to break through the music and he turned to see the beautiful bride with a young woman he'd not yet spotted among the reception guests.

"This is Maggie Malone," Vanessa introduced. "She's traveled all the way from Wickenburg to attend the reception."

"So this is the friend you're always talking about," Cordell said, while trying not to stare at Vanessa's friend.

The petite woman had a cloud of vivid red-gold hair that waved from the crown of her head all the way to her waist, while green eyes, the color of rich emeralds, were sliding over his face in a surreptitious way.

"Right. And she only arrived an hour ago," Vanessa explained. "So far she's met your parents and Jack, but not the rest of the family. I thought I'd start with you."

"Nice of you to put me at the head of introductions, Van," he said with a playful grin. "Or was it a case of getting the worst over first?"

Vanessa laughed. "Don't be silly. Everyone in Jack's family is the best."

"Van, you're a perfect diplomat." He offered his hand to the red-haired beauty. "Hello, Maggie. Nice to meet you."

"Cord is foreman of Stone Creek Ranch," Vanessa informed her. "And the middle child of the family, which makes him younger than Jack."

Cordell leveled a playful smile at Maggie. "Five years younger to be exact. I'm also better looking and smarter than Jack, too. But if you stick around for a while, you'll figure that out for yourself."

Vanessa winked at Maggie. "Never mind Cord. When you get past his nonsense you'll find he's actually a nice guy."

Maggie stepped slightly forward and placed her small hand in his. "It's a pleasure to meet you, Mr. Hollister."

Cordell quickly corrected her. "Sorry, it might get confusing if you called me Mr. Hollister. Counting Dad, there are six Mr. Hollisters here on the ranch. Better make it Cord."

She untangled her hand from his and while her gaze continued to sweep over his face, Cordell was amazed to feel a dull blush creeping up his neck. Women never made him self-conscious. But something about the little patronizing curve to her lips made him feel like an idiot.

"Cord it will be," she said.

"Maggie is an RN," Vanessa informed him. "She works the ER unit in a Wickenburg hospital. She's also single. But don't ask me how she hangs on to that status. I can't decide if she's stubborn or picky."

Maggie let out a good-natured groan. "Van, please—would you stop it! I—"

She was about to say more on the subject, but just then his mother walked up.

"Sorry for butting in, Van," Claire said. "But I have some old family friends over here who can't wait to meet you. Would you mind coming with me for a few minutes?"

"I'd love to, Claire." She looked at Maggie and Cordell. "Cord, would you mind introducing Maggie to the rest of the family?"

"I can't think of anything I'd rather do."

Cordell watched Vanessa and his mother disappear into the crowd, then glanced over at Maggie. Judging by the dubious look on her face, she wasn't exactly pleased to have him as her temporary host.

"Don't worry, Maggie. I don't bite. At least, not hard enough to hurt," he added with a wide grin.

"Thank you for that bit of information," she said. "You've put me completely at ease."

Her prim tone wasn't softened by a smile and he decided she must have already sized him up as someone she'd rather avoid. But that was hardly enough to stop him from taking a long, leisurely survey of her oval face.

"That was my sole intention, Maggie." He gestured to the crowd of dancers moving over the worn wood floor. "What do you think of Jack and Van's reception?"

"Everyone appears to be having a good time."

Everyone except her, Cordell thought. She wasn't smiling or tapping her toe to the beat of the lively music. She wasn't even trying to make polite conversation. Had the grim situations she encountered in the ER taken the joy out of her? No. He doubted that was the woman's problem. His older sister, Grace, was an MD and she'd seen plenty of trauma, but it hadn't soured her.

"Mom and Dad suggested having the belated wedding party at the civic center building in town, but Jack nixed that idea. He wanted the shindig here on the ranch and Van agreed. We spent more than a week cleaning out this hay barn to get it ready. Looks pretty good, don't you think? Or is it too rustic for a city girl like you?"

Cutting a glance up to his face, she quickly corrected, "I'm not a *city* girl. Wickenburg population is only in the four digits."

"Oh. Well, Stone Creek Ranch is miles away from everything," he explained. "Anything with more than two stoplights is like a city to me."

To his utter frustration, her expression remained stoic.

After a moment, she said, "You must not get out much."

Cordell couldn't help but burst out laughing and she reacted with a faint frown.

"You find that amusing?" she asked.

"Well, to hear my brothers tell it, I'm always going out. But usually Beaver or Cedar City is the extent of my travels. Guess you saw those towns on your way here."

She nodded. "Barely. Thunderstorms delayed my flight into Cedar City and then I had to wait for my rental car. I'm sure I broke the speed limit driving through Beaver, but I thought I was going to miss Jack and Van's reception entirely."

He smiled, while thinking her complexion was the perfect definition of peaches and cream with a dusting of golden freckles across the bridge of her nose. He figured her skin would feel smooth against his tongue, while her dark red lips would no doubt taste sweeter than a comb of wild honey. But he'd never get close enough to this stern little nurse to find out, he thought.

He said, "That would've been a shame. This is a nice party. Especially the music. The guys with the guitars and violins are all neighbors and the one on the keyboard plays piano at our church in Beaver."

She looked over to where the little band was currently whipping out a popular country tune. "Neighbors? I drove for miles and miles out here without spotting a single house."

His smile was indulgent. "We consider anyone

within a thirty-mile radius to be a neighbor. Otherwise, we wouldn't have any."

"Vanessa warned me that Stone Creek Ranch was even more isolated than the Hollisters' Three Rivers Ranch down in Arizona. I found that hard to believe. Until I started driving out here." She slanted a curious glance at him. "Were you surprised about Jack and Van eloping?"

Trying to steer his thoughts away from the tempting curve of her lips, he said, "Not really. Everyone in the family could see they were smitten with each other. Were you surprised that Van suddenly married?"

"In a way. But I was happy. She deserves the best and your brother obviously adores her."

"That's an understatement." He gestured toward a long table laden with an assortment of drinks and a massive tiered wedding cake. "Have you had cake and champagne yet?"

"Not yet."

While she focused on the milling crowd, Cordell allowed his gaze to drop to her dress. The midnight blue garment was fashioned with a turtleneck and long tight sleeves and though it didn't reveal any skin, the shimmery fabric clung to her slender curves like a glove. Normally, he was attracted to women with more flesh to their figures, so why was he feeling the urge to wrap his hands around her tiny waist?

Clearing his throat, he said, "Let's go over and get a glass of champagne. Afterward, we'll weave our way through the crowd and I'll introduce you to my brothers and sisters."

"I, uh, think I should wait. Van might be back any minute."

Her reluctant attitude mystified him. "I doubt she'll show up anytime soon. She's the queen of this ball, so to speak, her attention is going to be divided. And she did tell me to keep you company."

She glanced away from him. "That was just a figure of speech."

Cordell was beginning to get annoyed with her, but did his best not to show it. He didn't want to hurt Vanessa by insulting her friend.

"Okay. We'll skip the champagne. Let's go find my siblings. Hopefully you'll like them a bit better than you like me."

Surprise widened her eyes. "We just met. And you've already decided that I don't like you?"

"Forget I said that." He reached for her arm and was relieved when she didn't pull away from him. "I see Hunter helping himself to a piece of cake. Have you met him yet?"

"No. Is he a Hollister?" she asked, as he ushered her toward the refreshment table.

"The firstborn of us kids. In case Van hasn't told you, he owns and operates the Flying H Rodeo company."

"Sounds interesting. He must lead an exciting life," she replied.

"Compared to the rest of us, I suppose he does. But the grueling travel would get to me."

As they walked the short distance to where Hunter was standing, Cordell noticed a portion of her creamy thigh was exposed by a slit on the side of her dress and the scent drifting from her skin was wild and tangy, like the smell of the desert on a hot, dark night.

Yeah, she was sexy, all right, Cordell thought. But she also had hands-off written all over her. Which was probably a good thing. He didn't need to get mixed up with a woman right now. Hardly a month had passed since he'd gotten himself out of a messy entanglement with a brunette down in Parowan. He needed to steer clear of women for a while.

When Hunter spotted the two of them angling toward him, the rugged cowboy with rusty brown hair and a set of wide shoulders placed his plate of cake on the table and stepped out to meet them.

"Meet Van's friend from Wickenburg," Cord said to his brother. "This is Maggie Malone. She's a nurse. And don't suddenly develop a fever. She's here to enjoy the party."

Hunter reached out to shake Maggie's hand. "My pleasure, Ms. Malone. Welcome to Stone Creek Ranch."

Maggie shook Hunter's hand and Cordell couldn't help but notice she gave him a wide, warm smile. Hell, what did Hunter have that he didn't? Maybe she went for older men. At thirty-nine, Hunter wasn't exactly old, but Cordell figured he was at least twelve or thirteen years older than Maggie.

"Thank you," she said. "I'm looking forward to seeing the place in the daylight hours."

"Do you plan to stay on the ranch for a while?" Hunter asked. "We always enjoy having company for Thanksgiving."

"How would you know?" Cordell shot the question at his brother. "You're rarely ever around for the holidays."

Hunter leveled a shrewd smile at him. "I didn't realize you missed me so much, Cord."

Cordell looked over to see Maggie's gaze vacillating between him and Hunter. Their subtle jabs at each other probably had had her wondering about their relationship. Cordell could've told her that he was tightly bonded to Hunter and all his brothers. They might argue at times, but the love between was enduring.

She said to Hunter, "Unfortunately, I can only stay a few days. I have to return to work before Thanksgiving."

"That's a shame. But it's good you and Van will have a bit of time to together," Hunter replied. "I imagine she's excited to show you the house she and Jack are having built."

Maggie said, "She's looking forward to having her own place. Not that she doesn't enjoy living in the big ranch house with everyone. But—"

"Newlyweds need privacy," Hunter finished for her.

Feeling the need to make his presence known, Cordell said, "Maggie has the notion you lead an exciting life, Hunter. She'd probably enjoy a few of your rodeo stories."

Hunter grimaced and Cordell figured this evening had to be a strain for his older brother. Being reminded of his failed marriage had to be rough. Especially when Hunter had never gotten over his wife's leaving. Which made no sense to Cordell. In his opinion, Hunter's wife didn't deserve to be remembered.

Hunter focused on the crowd of dancing couples. "I wouldn't dream of boring Maggie with that stuff."

"Not all women find rodeos boring," Cordell felt compelled to say.

Hunter leveled a meaningful look at him. "Thanks for the reminder, Cord. Now if both of you will excuse me, I see someone I need to go say hello to."

As Hunter walked away, he noticed Maggie staring after him.

She said, "I get the feeling you ruffled his feathers—on purpose. Do you enjoy goading your brother?"

Cordell grimaced. "Not really. I did it for a good reason. You have to trust me on that."

Her short laugh caused him to stare at her in wonder. "You find that funny?"

For the first time this evening, she smiled at him. "The idea of trusting you is very funny."

He playfully slapped a hand over his heart. "Van described you as a sweetheart. She didn't mention you had claws."

She gave him another dimpled smile that caused something to quiver deep in his gut.

"Van is too nice to say bad things about anyone," she said, then surprised him once again by curving her arm lightly through his. "Shall we go find your other siblings? I can't wait to see if any of them are like you."

He very much wanted to place his hand over the one she had resting on his forearm, but decided not to press his luck. "I'll save you the disappointment and tell you that none of my siblings are like me."

"I'm sure your parents are relieved about that."

He chuckled and as he guided her across the wide expanse of barn floor to where his younger brother Flint was standing, he forgot the party was a wedding reception. He even forgot about his plan to avoid women for a while. Cordell had always been a man to live for the pleasure of the moment and he didn't see any good reason to break the habit tonight.

Why couldn't she quit staring at Cordell Hollister?

The question continued to nag at Maggie as she sat on a hay bale covered with a bright serape and sipped champagne from a stemmed glass. Vanessa's twin sisters-in-law, Bonnie and Beatrice, were seated on either side of her, but Maggie was digesting only half of the young women's chatter. Her thoughts were consumed with the good-looking ranch foreman, who was currently waltzing a pretty brunette around the dance floor.

Before Vanessa had introduced her to Cordell,

she'd warned Maggie that he was a bit of a flirt. But she'd failed to mention anything about him having striking looks or that he oozed masculinity from every pore.

The moment he'd turned around and she'd found herself looking into his sky-blue eyes, she'd felt a jolt all the way to her feet. Which had been a ridiculous reaction, considering she was accustomed to seeing plenty of rugged and sexy cowboys. After all, Wickenburg was known as a cowboy town. But she'd never met one who looked exactly like Cordell.

He was six feet of hard, lean muscle with long legs and broad shoulders. Beneath his black Stetson, thick, sandy blond hair waved around his ears and down onto his neck. As for his face, it was made up of unyielding angles and a set of lips that looked just as hard as his squared chin.

Darn it! More than an hour had passed since Cordell had escorted her around the big barn and introduced her to his relatives. And when the two of them had eventually run onto Jack and Vanessa in the crowd, he'd excused himself and left her in their company.

At the time, she'd told herself she was relieved he'd parted ways with her. It had been a constant fight with herself to keep from staring at him and pretending he wasn't creating an earthquake inside of her. Now, after watching him dance with one woman after another, without so much as a glance in her direction, she was actually feeling disappointed. Which was a totally stupid reaction. She'd seen his kind before. He was as sexy as hell and he knew it. He used his charm to wrap women around his finger and then toss them away without the slightest prick to his conscience.

No. She didn't need the company of a man like him. She needed a man who was steady and true, a guy who wanted a family rather than a few romps in bed. So why did she keep looking at him and wondering how it would feel to dance in his arms?

"Maggie, do you ever visit Three Rivers Ranch?"

Glad that Beatrice's question had interrupted her wandering thoughts, she looked over at the blonde twin. Except for being slightly shorter and smaller in stature, her features were almost identical to Bonnie's.

"On occasion. I'm friends with Camille. She's the youngest of the family."

"Oh. I was just wondering," Beatrice replied. "Jack said they have dozens of nice cowboys working on the place."

"And Bea wants to meet them all," Bonnie spoke with a roll of her eyes. "Just like they're better than the guys up here. I've tried to tell her a man is a man no matter where he is."

"And how would you know?" Beatrice fired the question back at her sister. "The only men you've ever dated are milksops and those have been few and far between."

"Is it a crime to like sensitive men?" Bonnie asked in a deceptively sweet voice.

"No. It's a bore," Beatrice answered between sips

of champagne. "But you don't mind being bored. All that concerns you is feeling safe."

Bonnie gave her sister a hard look and Maggie was beginning to fear the two were going to end up in a heated argument, but before the conversation could go any further, a young man wearing a dark Western suit walked up and asked Beatrice for a dance.

As the two of them walked away, Maggie couldn't help saying, "I guess you and your twin don't always see eye to eye."

To her surprise, Bonnie smiled and shrugged. "Mom says Bea and I argued with each other before we could walk. We look alike but we're totally unalike in personalities. But we have a fierce love for each other. It's hard to explain. Other than we have a twin thing. Do you have sisters or brothers, Maggie?"

Shaking her head, she said, "Unfortunately, no. My mother passed away when I was five. And I was her only child."

"Oh, that's sad."

"Yes, but I had a wonderful mother for a while," Maggie said gently. "That's better than having a bad one for years and years. As for my father, I never knew him."

Bonnie looked at her with regret. "I'm sorry to hear that. I've been blessed with great parents, so I try to never take their presence for granted."

Maggie nodded while thinking Bonnie had hit the nail squarely on the head when she'd said her and Beatrice had totally different personalities. The twins were only twenty-four, two years younger than

Maggie, yet Bonnie talked like an old soul, whereas Beatrice seemed much younger—and eager to spread her wings.

"I hate to interrupt such a deep conversation, but I've not had a dance with you, Maggie. Would you like to take a whirl?"

She glanced around to see Cordell standing directly in front of her chair and her heart instantly reacted with a hard lurch.

"I'm not really much of a dancer," she told him.

He brushed aside her flimsy excuse. "I saw you dancing earlier with Hunter and he wasn't limping off the floor when the song ended."

Surprised that he'd even noticed, she said, "I think Hunter is wearing steel-toed boots."

He laughed and Bonnie chuckled softly.

"Hunter has never owned a pair of steel-toed boots in his life." He reached his hand down to her. "Come on. This is a slow song. You won't have to do much."

No, she thought, she'd only have to stand in his arms and pretend she was as cool as the north wind blowing outside the barn, when she'd actually be melting like an icicle on a hot June day.

Seeing no polite way to avoid him, she placed her champagne glass on the empty spot next to her, then taking his hand, rose from the chair.

"Excuse me, Bonnie."

"Sure," the young woman replied.

As Cordell led her among the dancing couples, Maggie said, "If you were worried I was feeling like a wallflower you shouldn't have bothered with the dance invitation. I was thoroughly enjoying your sisters."

"You, a wallflower?" He followed the question with a laugh. "You know, Maggie, you're terribly funny. I'll bet you keep all your patients laughing."

"The ones who are fortunate enough to be breathing."

He laughed again, but the smile on his face sobered as he drew her into his arms. "Sorry. I didn't mean that to sound like your job is funny. I'm sure it's very stressful and emotional."

It was difficult for Maggie to digest his serious comment when the contact of his hard body was causing her mind to buzz like a high voltage wire.

"It's both. But thankfully every situation isn't serious."

"Do you like your job?" he asked.

"Love it."

He smelled like the wind that had touched her face the moment she'd stood outside the car in front of the ranch house. The scent was a unique mixture of sage and juniper and some sort of grass. It was a wild, rugged smell that underscored the fact that he was all man.

"Is nursing something you decided on after you became an adult?" he asked curiously. "Or was it always a goal to be an RN?"

"My mother was very ill for a long while before she passed on. I was five years old at the time and the nurses who cared for her were the people who reassured me and saw that my needs were met. I decided then that I wanted to grow up and help people feel better."

"I wish I could say I had an admirable motive to do what I do. But I can't. Being the foreman of Stone Creek Ranch is something I do for a purely selfish reason. I love the work and I want this place to be around whenever my brothers and I get older."

Maybe it was her imagination, but the music seemed to be getting slower. Since he'd circled his arm around the back of her waist and pulled her close against, she doubted they'd traveled more than three feet.

"Working for a united family effort is admirable, too," she told him.

His blue gaze dropped to her face and Maggie had the strangest urge to moisten her lips with the tip of her tongue.

"You think so?" He shrugged one shoulder. "Sometimes I feel guilty because the ranch is something that's always been here. Our father and grandfather are the ones who really toiled and sweated to make the land what it is today."

"But you help keep the ranch going," she pointed out.

"I try. And Jack is great at helping Dad manage everything."

"How did you end up with the foreman job?"

He grinned and she found herself gazing in fascination at his white teeth and the little crinkles at the corners of his eyes. Did he have any idea what kind of effect he had on women? She suspected he might, based on Van's warning.

"I just naturally like giving orders," he said.

She looked away and reminded herself to breathe. Otherwise she was going to embarrass herself by wilting into a heap at his feet.

"I imagine there's more to your job than giving orders," she replied.

"Dad believes I know more about caring for livestock. And that's a never-ending job around here."

The song came to an end and Maggie was trying to decide whether she was disappointed or relieved, when he said, "Let's dance this next one."

Her senses were already a wreck. Five more minutes in his arms and she'd probably start babbling nonsense. "I really should—"

"You really should dance with me, Maggie," a male voice behind her said. "No need in Cord having all the fun."

Maggie caught sight of Cordell's frown as she turned to see the voice belonged to Quint, the youngest brother of the Hollister clan. Earlier, Cord had introduced them.

"You always have to be a pest, baby brother," Cordell said with a good-natured groan, then added, "Thanks for the dance, Maggie. It was a pleasure."

Maggie watched him disappear into the crowd of dancers, while standing at her side, Quint said, "You shouldn't give Cord a second glance, Maggie. He's no good."

Dismayed, she looked at the young cowboy. "That's a harsh thing to say about your brother."

"I'd better rephrase it. Cord is a good guy. He's just no good where ladies like you are concerned. He considers breaking hearts a form of entertainment."

She'd already concluded that Cordell was a playboy. But to hear Quint say it made her wonder if there was a streak of jealousy involved.

"Thanks for the warning, Quint, but I'm only going to be here on the ranch for a few days."

Quint's short laugh was full of sarcasm. "One day is more than enough time for Cord to do damage."

Before Maggie could assure him that she had no intentions of letting Cordell near her heart or any other part of her anatomy, the music suddenly started and Quint led her off into a quick two-step.

The young cowboy was smooth on his feet and Maggie had to focus to keep up with him and the beat of the music, yet even as she danced, her thoughts strayed to Cordell and the strong reaction she'd felt when his arm had pulled her close and his eyes had glinted with sinful promises.

And as she automatically twirled beneath Quint's arm, she realized that Cordell didn't need one day to cast a spell over a woman. He'd managed to captivate her in one short evening.

But tomorrow would be different, Maggie promised herself. Tomorrow she'd have her senses back in good working order and she was going to make darned sure she kept a safe distance from the foreman of Stone Creek Ranch.

Chapter Two

"I didn't know it was supposed to snow today. I'm glad I wore my oilskin."

Cordell glanced over at Quint as the two men rode their horses slowly through the snow-dusted sage toward the foothills lying north of the ranch. This morning, with the weather predicted to worsen through the day, they needed to make sure all the cow-calf pairs were off the mountain and on to a place where the animals could shelter. To help with the chore, Cordell had sent three of the five ranch hands to search the eastern range, while the other two hands were busy putting out feed and hay.

"There is such a thing as a weather forecast. If you'd remember to check it, you might know how to dress in the morning," Cordell told him.

Quint grunted and hunched deeper down in the saddle. "Who needs a weatherman to tell him it's going to be cold or wet? I have two eyes. I can look at the sky."

"Okay. You lucked out today and wore your duster."

A smug smile crossed Quint's face. "I lucked out last night, too. Van's pretty little friend danced three dances with me."

"I never noticed," Cordell said.

"Liar. I saw you watching us," Quint gloated. "Jealous, weren't you?"

Cordell let out a short laugh. "Why would I be jealous? I danced with a number of pretty women at the reception last night."

"Yeah. But none of them looked like Maggie. You know, I never thought I'd go for a redhead, but she's a real firecracker. And she's the same age as me. You know what that means, don't you?"

"Yeah. You're way too young to be thinking about women," Cordell muttered.

"No. It means she's way too young for you, brother."

Cordell kept his gaze focused on his horse's ears, while thinking Quint was right. Maggie was too young and definitely too aloof for his taste. Now, if he could just convince himself of that, until her stay on the ranch was over, he'd be a smart man.

"Probably so," he said as he reached forward and brushed away the flakes of snow collecting on the horse's black mane. "And now that you have those bits of wisdom off your chest, do you think you can get your mind back to punching cows?"

"Punching cows? Hell, we'll have to ride two more miles before we ever see a cow," Quint muttered. "I don't know why you didn't let me stay behind with Jett. I could've helped him fill molasses licks and Brooks could've come with you. He's better at herding cattle than me, anyway."

"Yeah, he is. But I wanted to hear you gripe all morning. Makes my day extra nice to know I'm making you miserable."

He glanced over to see Quint had lowered the brim of his hat to shield the blowing snow from his face. His younger brother was always complaining about the hard work, yet he continued to stay on the ranch and follow orders.

"You know, sometimes I wonder if I have good sense," Quint said as the horses continued to pick their way over the frozen ground. "With my degree, I could be teaching high school agriculture."

"Then why don't you? You talk about it often enough."

"Because I'd hate being cooped up in a room all day."

In spite of the miserable conditions, Cordell had to laugh. "You're outside now. You should be happy," he said, then added slyly, "I probably shouldn't mention this. But Dad is going to put you in charge of the sheep production."

He glanced over just as Quint shot straight up in the saddle and stared at Cord in dazed wonder.

"Are you kidding me?" he asked.

"No. Jack told me yesterday, so I expect Dad will be talking to you about the job in the next day or two. Why? Don't you like the idea? Or you think it's too much responsibility for you?"

"Well, shoot no! I can handle the job just fine." He squared his shoulders and flashed Cordell a toothy grin. "Guess Dad finally realized I was worth something around here."

Funny how one positive accomplishment could make a man's whole world seem brighter, even on a snowy day, Cord thought.

"He sees your hard work and it's paid off. You'll be good with the sheep, Quint. You know a heck of a lot more about them than I do."

If possible, Quint looked even more surprised. "You mean that?"

"I really do."

"Thanks, brother. Coming from you that means a lot," Quint said, then added sheepishly, "And Cord, all that stuff about Maggie—I was just trying to get your goat. Yeah, she danced with me, but all the time I could tell she was thinking about you. Darn it."

The redheaded nurse wasn't a firecracker like Quint had described her, Cordell thought. She was more like a red Popsicle—sweet but so cold a bite of her would make his teeth ache.

"How could you possibly know what she was thinking?" Cordell asked. "Don't tell me you asked her."

"I'm not that dumb. I could just tell by the look on her face every time she spotted you. Her lips flattened and her eyes narrowed."

"You mean like a woman looks whenever she's plotting murder. Well, thanks for the warning, brother. Whenever she's around I'll be sure and watch my back."

"It's not your back you ought to be worried about, Cord. She's the kind that could get under your skin."

Cordell's short laugh was carried away with the cold wind. "Not my skin. My hide is way too tough for that to happen."

Last night, when Maggie had first arrived on Stone Creek Ranch, it had been dark and the only things she could see about the house was that the sizable structure consisted of two stories, countless windows and a tall rock chimney towering up over the north side of the roof. Large round rock formed the foundation and continued half way up the outer wall of the bottom story, while the remaining walls consisted of board lapped siding painted a soft gray.

Later, after the party had ended, she'd been too tired to do more than climb the stairs to the room Van and Claire had shown her to and fall into bed. Now, with the gray morning light slanting through the window, she hurriedly threw a thick robe over her pajamas and made her way out of the bedroom and on to the staircase.

Along the way, she noticed there was no sight of

anyone moving about on the second floor, nor any sound coming from the floor below. From what little she knew of ranching life, eight o'clock was the middle of the morning for ranching people. However, with the reception going on into the wee hours, she'd assumed the family would sleep late. And perhaps they were, she thought, as she glanced in passing at several closed doors.

Careful to keep her steps noiseless, she made her way down the wide staircase, while thinking the Hollister home had obviously been built many years ago, when woodwork had been painstakingly carved by hand. The beautiful craftsmanship was evident in the balustrade lining the stairs and the tongue-and-groove walls that were painted a soothing sand color. The oak flooring gleamed with a soft patina and as she reached the bottom floor landing, she caught the scent of lemon wax mixed with the faint smell of roses.

Since Vanessa had moved here to Stone Creek Ranch, she'd never made mention of this house having subtle similarities to the Three Rivers Ranch house. Maybe her friend hadn't noticed the vague parallels, but Maggie was seeing them. True, the Hollisters' house in Arizona had three stories and was somewhat larger; however, this one was of a significant size and the interior was very reminiscent of the other. Which was strange, indeed, given the fact that the two families hadn't known they were related until a few short months ago.

She was nearing the kitchen when the faint scent of bacon and sausage drifted to her and as she entered the door, she expected to find some of the family eating breakfast. Instead, Claire was the only one in the room. She was standing at the cabinet counter stirring something in a big aluminum mixing bowl.

She looked up as Maggie joined her. "Good morning, Maggie. Ready for coffee and breakfast?"

"Is that what you're preparing?"

Claire gave her an indulgent smile. "No. I'm afraid you missed the regular breakfast. This is sourdough mix. I don't know if you're familiar with sourdough, but you have to keep adding ingredients to keep it going. It'll be ready for biscuits tomorrow morning."

Maggie groaned with misgivings. "Everyone had such a late night I thought you were all in bed and I was getting up early."

Claire chuckled. "Ranching folks don't get the luxury of sleeping late. Unless someone is sick. And even then, we try to drag ourselves out of bed. Livestock always needs tending. And I have working men to feed."

Maggie watched Claire continue to push the wooden spoon through the dough. "You don't have house help?"

"A young woman comes in once a week to help with the deep cleaning. Otherwise, the twins and I do everything. I take care of most all the cooking. Sometimes Bonnie helps prepare the meals. She's pretty good at cooking. Van tries, but she needs practice. Bea can barely make a boiled egg, so she helps with the cleaning up. And believe it or not, sometimes the guys will lend a hand in the kitchen."

Maggie couldn't imagine Cordell washing a dish or scraping scraps from a plate, but she kept the thought to herself. "You've obviously raised your children right."

"Well, we're a big family. So we all have to pitch in." Claire glanced at her. "Jack and Van tell me that the Hollisters down in Arizona have two cooks and a housekeeper, plus a cook for the bunkhouse."

"They do. The ranch is massive. And the family is growing, so they even have a nanny for the children now."

Shaking her head with wonder, Claire said, "I've visited with Maureen over the phone and she's told me about all her grandchildren. I can't relate. Not yet, at least. I only have one grandchild. Grace's son, Ross. But I expect that will soon change now that Van and Jack are married."

As longtime friends, Maggie and Vanessa had often talked about how much they each wanted children. Now that she'd married Jack, Vanessa's dream for a family would soon be coming true. As for Maggie, her luck with men had never been good. She couldn't see a husband on her horizon, much less a baby.

"I hope so. Van and Jack will make great parents."

"Hadley and I think so, too. And in case you didn't

get a chance to meet Hadley last night, he's my husband and the children's father."

"Actually, Van did introduce me to Hadley. He's a charming man."

"I've heard that before," Claire said with a chuckle, then setting the spoon aside, she covered the top of the bowl with plastic wrap. "There. Let me put this in the fridge and I'll fix you something to eat."

"Please, don't bother. Coffee will be enough. And anyway, I don't normally eat much in the mornings."

"Nonsense. It's no bother." Claire placed the sourdough mix into a huge stainless-steel refrigerator, then walked to the end of the cabinet where a coffee machine held a glass carafe half full of coffee.

"Do you cook?" Claire asked, then laughed lightly as she filled an orange-and-gold-patterned mug with coffee. "My daughters would shame me for asking you that question. They say nowadays it isn't important if a woman can cook."

"I don't mind you asking. And I'll admit I'm not too good at cooking. My breakfasts usually consist of cold cereal and dinners are mostly something from the store that's already put together."

"Nothing wrong with that. You're a busy woman." Claire handed Maggie the mug and a spoon, then gestured to a sugar bowl and tiny pitcher of cream sitting in the middle of the table. "Sit down with your coffee and I'll fix you something. I have plenty of bread and jam if you'd like toast."

Maggie gave her a grateful smile. "Toast sounds wonderful."

While Claire dropped bread into the toaster, Maggie took a seat at the long table and stirred a dollop of cream into her coffee,

"Where's Vanessa?"

"She said to tell you she'd be in her office upstairs."

Back in late July, Maureen Hollister had hired Vanessa to dig into their family tree. During her work for the Arizona Hollister matriarch, an intriguing possibility arose of the two Hollister families being related. After a DNA test confirmed her suspicion, Vanessa had continued her search—now at Stone Creek—to unravel the family mystery, but so far she hadn't found any definite link.

Maggie took a careful sip of the hot coffee. "She's working on the family tree today?"

Claire glanced over her shoulder and smiled at Maggie. "She only planned to work until you got up."

Maggie hadn't taken the time to brush her hair. Now she shook back the tangled mass. "I should've set the alarm."

Claire carried a small plate with two slices of toast and a jar of raspberry jam over to Maggie, then took a seat across from her.

"Van tells us that you've worked in the ER for a long while now."

Maggie slathered a piece of the toast with a thick layer of jam. "Five years. Ever since I became an RN."

"Sometimes I worry Grace will burn out," Claire said thoughtfully. "Being one of the few doctors in town, she's overloaded with work. I would understand if she decided to shut the door on her clinic and just walk away. But she's not that type of person. She cares too much."

Last night at the reception, Maggie had met Grace, the doctor of the family. The pretty blonde resembled her mother, only Grace was considerably taller and her eyes were green whereas Claire's were blue.

Maggie said, "I understand. The ones who care too much are the ones who carry the heaviest loads."

"Yes," Claire replied. "Caring often comes with a heavy price."

Maggie wondered if the Hollister matriarch was talking about Grace or someone else in the family. Had Cordell ever paid a price for caring too much? Somehow she doubted it. She couldn't imagine the man agonizing over anyone, except himself. But then, she didn't really know him well enough to pass any kind of judgment on his character. And besides, she'd be going home in a few short days. Nothing about Cordell Hollister should matter to her.

After Maggie finished her toast and coffee, she returned to her bedroom and dressed in jeans and a warm sweater, then made her way to Vanessa's office, which was located on the west end of the second floor.

When she stepped through the open doorway, she

immediately spotted her friend sitting behind a desk, peering intently at a monitor screen.

"Good morning, Mrs. Hollister. Am I interrupting?"

Glancing away from the monitor, Vanessa gave her a cheery smile. "Well, Sleeping Beauty has finally awoken."

Smiling sheepishly, Maggie said, "I should have known you all got up with the chickens. I felt like an idiot for showing up in the kitchen long after everyone had eaten."

Vanessa waved away her words. "Don't be silly. You can sleep until noon if you like."

Maggie turned a full circle as she took in her friend's work area. "This is nice, Van."

"Claire and Hadley fixed this room for me before I first came to Stone Creek. They thought I needed a quiet place to work."

"To go to the trouble and expense of making you an office, they must feel very strongly about uncovering all the branches to the Hollister family tree."

Vanessa leaned back in her chair. "They're very serious about it. Most everyone in the two families wants to know how they came to be related."

"Hmm. I'm not sure I'd want to know anything about my family on the paternal side."

With her father walking out before she'd ever been born, Maggie knew nothing about the man. One of her mother's friends told Maggie he'd originally come from Bishop, California, but after twenty-six years that hardly meant anything.

Vanessa thoughtfully tapped a pencil against the mouse pad on her desk. "Have you ever thought about the possibility of having half siblings somewhere? It might be nice for you to meet them."

Maggie grimaced. "So I could tell them what a creep their father is, or was? No thanks, Van. I'm okay as I am."

Vanessa shook her head. "But you have no one. Except the aunt and uncle who took you in when your mother died. And they're not exactly a loving family unit. I think—"

Maggie held up a hand to prevent her from saying more. "Van, please drop it, will you? I don't want to start my day on a sour note."

Vanessa gave her an apologetic smile. "Right. I'm done. So have you had coffee? Something to eat?"

"Oh, yes. Claire fixed me a plate of toast and we had a nice visit. Your mother-in-law is a lovely woman, Van. Actually, I'm amazed that she gave birth to eight healthy children."

Vanessa nodded. "Funny, but when I first met Jack, he described his mother as being very fragile. Maybe in stature, but she's anything but fragile otherwise. I can only hope I can be as strong a mother and wife as she is."

"No need for you to worry. You're going to be great at both." Maggie walked over to a small window on the left side of the room and glanced out at the view. The November sky was gray with bits of snow landing against the glass panes. But the wintry weather didn't diminish the beauty of the sweeping landscape of Stone Creek Ranch. "It's snowing, Van!"

"Yes. I looked out the window earlier. Winter has apparently arrived in this part of Utah."

Maggie continued to gaze out the window. "This view is something else. The valley looks like it goes for miles before it reaches the mountains."

"Jack and his family call the nearest peak Snow Mountain. I'm not sure if that's its official name on the map, but since the mountain is actually located on Stone Creek Ranch property I guess they can call it whatever they want."

Glancing at her friend, Maggie smiled with fond remembrance. "Remember when we were little girls and the closer it grew to Christmas the harder we'd wish for snow to fall? Wickenburg might see one or two flakes fly through the air in the dead of winter."

Vanessa chuckled. "I remember. We fantasized about making a snowman and going sledding."

Turning her gaze back to the view beyond the window, Maggie dropped her focus directly to the yard behind the house. Along with an open patch of brown grass and a fair-sized patio, there was a low stone fence built along the outside edge of the yard. Next to it, some sort of shrubs had been covered to prevent them from freezing. "What's beneath the gray tarps?"

"Tea roses."

Surprised, Maggie said, "I wouldn't have thought of growing tea roses here in this mountain climate. But I don't suppose it's any stranger than all the irises Tess has growing in the front yard of the Bar X down in Arizona."

Vanessa said, "I was told Jack's grandfather Lionel planted them in honor of his mother. He kept them perfectly cultivated until he passed away. Nowadays Claire tends to the roses. From what I gather, she was especially close to her father-in-law."

"Last night at the reception I noticed you seem to be especially close to your father-in-law," Maggie said with a faint smile. "Lucky you that you have such great in-laws."

Her smile full of affection, Vanessa said, "Hadley is a big teddy bear. And I'll always be grateful he literally forced Jack and I to face each other and admit our love. Otherwise, I might have gone back to Wickenburg and never seen Jack again."

Maggie stepped away from the window and walked over to Vanessa's desk. "And that would've been a tragedy," she said, then gestured to a nearby stack of cardboard boxes. "What's all that stuff? I thought you were doing all your genealogy search on the computer."

"I am researching all I can on the internet. But I'm also going through boxes of old documents and papers that's been stored away for years. I need to find something to give me a clue as to when Hadley's father, Lionel, was born. So far I'm stuck."

"I'd love to help you," Maggie said eagerly. "And from the sizes of those boxes, it looks like you could use an extra pair of eyes."

"Thanks. But you didn't come all the way up here to dig through a bunch of old dusty papers."

Maggie dismissed her words with the wave of a hand. "No. I came up here for your wedding reception. Now that it's over I need to make myself useful."

A dreamy smile appeared on Vanessa's face. "I thought our reception was perfect. Did you enjoy the evening?"

Maggie had enjoyed everything about the evening, except her preoccupation with Cordell. Once she'd met him, she'd had trouble focusing on anything else.

"It was lovely, Van. I'll admit it was the first reception I've ever attended that was held in a barn. But it was the perfect setting for you and Jack."

Vanessa laughed softly. "Jack says he's turned me into a hayseed like him. But you know what? I wouldn't want to be anything else. Guess being in love makes a woman see everything differently."

Maggie glanced away from her friend's face. "I'm beginning to doubt I'll ever know the feeling of being in love."

"Maggie, that's an odd thing for you to say. I got the impression you were in love with Dr. Sheridan—that is, before he left town. But the way I remember things, he asked you to go with him. And you refused."

"I had to refuse," Maggie said ruefully. "Because

deep down our relationship didn't feel right to me. Something was missing. Passion—electricity—I don't know exactly."

She glanced over to see Vanessa was studying her thoughtfully.

"So what did you think about Cord?" she asked. "I got the feeling he wasn't quite what you expected."

Maggie didn't want to discuss Cordell. She wanted to forget him. But admitting such things to Vanessa would only create suspicion and more questions from her friend.

"I wasn't expecting him to be such a sexy devil. You should've warned me beforehand."

Smiling cleverly, Vanessa said, "Why? Then I would've had to warn you about all the Hollister brothers. They're all striking men in their own way."

Maggie sighed. "True. But there's something about Cord—well, he's not like his brothers."

"They're all different," Vanessa agreed. "That's something I learned right off."

Different. Oh yes, Cordell was that and so much more. "Cord's brothers are all gentlemen. But he's—"

Vanessa's eyes narrowed. "Did he insult you, or something?"

No. Worse than that, Maggie thought. He'd put some sort of crazy spell on her and she wasn't sure she was over it yet.

Moving away from Vanessa's desk, Maggie ambled aimlessly back over to the window. "No. He was polite. But he was an incessant flirt."

Vanessa's laugh pulled Maggie's gaze away from the view of Snow Mountain and back to her friend.

"What's so funny?"

Vanessa continued to chuckle. "I didn't know it was a crime for a man to flirt with a woman."

Unable to hide her annoyance, Maggie said, "I didn't call him a criminal."

"But you think he is. Because he rubbed you the wrong way. Right?"

Maggie scowled at her. "He didn't rub me *any* way."

"Maybe you would've enjoyed him more if he had," Vanessa suggested with an impish grin.

Maggie let out a rueful groan. "Okay, I'll admit it. Cord rattled me—because I wasn't expecting to be attracted to him. But I was. And that makes me feel darned stupid."

"Oh Maggie, why feel stupid for reacting like a normal woman?" Vanessa asked with gentle reproach.

Maggie darted her friend a hopeless glance. "I suppose I don't like being one of a crowd. I know his kind, Van. That's why it was silly of me to be drawn to him."

Frowning thoughtfully, Vanessa said, "You're being hard on yourself for no reason. And I think you're being a bit hard on Cord, too. Yes, he's dated plenty of women and yes, he's a flirt. But deep down he'd give the shirt off his back to a friend in need. And like Jack, he's devoted to his family and this ranch. So he does have some good qualities."

Maggie gave her friend a lopsided smile. "I'm sure he does. I like to think we all do."

Smiling happily, Vanessa stood and joined her at the window. "Good. Now that we have that out of the way, let's drive over to the house site. It's really cold today, but the carpenters are working inside now and they'll have a few space heaters going. We shouldn't freeze while I'm showing you around."

"Don't worry about me getting cold. I bought all kinds of warm outerwear for this trip. And these next few days will probably be the only chance I'll ever get to use them."

Besides, if she started to shiver from the cold, Maggie thought, she'd only have to think about Cordell and her whole body would light up like a burning match to a gas-soaked log.

COMING NEXT MONTH FROM

HARLEQUIN®

SPECIAL EDITION™

#2971 FORTUNE'S FATHERHOOD DARE

The Fortunes of Texas: Hitting the Jackpot • by Makenna Lee

When bartender Damon Fortune Maloney boasts that he can handle any kid, single mom Sari Keeling dares him to watch her two rambunctious boys for just one day. It's game on, but Damon soon discovers that parenthood is tougher than he thought—and so is resisting Sari.

#2972 HER MAN OF HONOR

Love, Unveiled • by Teri Wilson

Bridal-advice columnist and jilted bride Everly England couldn't have predicted the feelings a sympathetic kiss from her best friend would ignite in her. Henry Aston knows the glamorous city girl is terrified romance will ruin their friendship. But this stand-in groom plans to win her "I do" after all!

#2973 MEETING HIS SECRET DAUGHTER

Forever, Texas • by Marie Ferrarella

When nurse Riley Robertson brought engineer Matt O'Brien to Forever to meet the daughter he never knew he had, she was only planning to help Matt see that he can be the father his little girl needs. But could the charming new dad be the man Riley didn't know she needed? And are the three ready to become a forever family?

#2974 THE RANCHER'S BABY

Aspen Creek Bachelors • by Kathy Douglass

Suddenly named guardian of a baby girl, rancher Isaac Montgomery gamely steps up for daddy duty, with the help of new neighbor Savannah Rogers. Sparks fly, but Savannah's reserved even as their feelings heat up. Are Isaac and his baby too painful a reminder of her heartbreaking loss? Or do they hold the key to healing?

#2975 ALL'S FAIR IN LOVE AND WINE

Love in the Valley • by Michele Dunaway

Unexpectedly back in town, Jack Clayton is acting as if he never crushed Sierra James's teenage heart. When he offers to buy her family's vineyard, the former navy lieutenant knows Jack is turning on the charm, but no way is she planning to melt for him again. But will denying what she still feels for Jack prove to be a victory she can savor?

#2976 NO RINGS ATTACHED

Once Upon a Wedding • by Mona Shroff

Fleeing her own nuptials wasn't part of wedding planner Sangeeta Parikh's plan. Neither was stumbling into chef Sonny Pandya's arms and becoming an internet sensation! So why not fake a relationship so Sangeeta can save face and her job, and to get Sonny much-needed exposure for his restaurant? It's a good plan for two commitmentphobes...until their fake commitment starts to feel all too real.

YOU CAN FIND MORE INFORMATION ON UPCOMING HARLEQUIN TITLES, FREE EXCERPTS AND MORE AT HARLEQUIN.COM.

HSECNM0223

Get 4 FREE REWARDS!
We'll send you 2 FREE Books plus 2 FREE Mystery Gifts.
Secret under the Stars
ELIZABETH BEVARLY
The Maverick's Marriage Pact
STELLA BAGWELL
The Cowboy's Ranch Rescue
Lisa Childs
His Partnership Proposal
FREE Value Over $20
Both the Harlequin® Special Edition and Harlequin® Heartwarming™ series feature compelling novels filled with stories of love and strength where the bonds of friendship, family and community unite.
YES! Please send me 2 FREE novels from the Harlequin Special Edition or Harlequin Heartwarming series and my 2 FREE gifts (gifts are worth about $10 retail). After receiving them, if I don't wish to receive any more books, I can return the shipping statement marked "cancel." If I don't cancel, I will receive 6 brand-new Harlequin Special Edition books every month and be billed just $5.49 each in the U.S. or $6.24 each in Canada, a savings of at least 12% off the cover price, or 4 brand-new Harlequin Heartwarming Larger-Print books every month and be billed just $6.24 each in the U.S. or $6.74 each in Canada, a savings of at least 19% off the cover price. It's quite a bargain! Shipping and handling is just 50¢ per book in the U.S. and $1.25 per book in Canada.* I understand that accepting the 2 free books and gifts places me under no obligation to buy anything. I can always return a shipment and cancel at any time by calling the number below. The free books and gifts are mine to keep no matter what I decide.
Choose one: ☐ Harlequin Special Edition (235/335 HDN GRJV) ☐ Harlequin Heartwarming Larger-Print (161/361 HDN GRJV)
Name (please print)
Address
Apt. #
City
State/Province
Zip/Postal Code
Email: Please check this box ☐ if you would like to receive newsletters and promotional emails from Harlequin Enterprises ULC and its affiliates. You can unsubscribe anytime.
Mail to the Harlequin Reader Service:
IN U.S.A.: P.O. Box 1341, Buffalo, NY 14240-8531
IN CANADA: P.O. Box 603, Fort Erie, Ontario L2A 5X3
Want to try 2 free books from another series? Call 1-800-873-8635 or visit www.ReaderService.com.
*Terms and prices subject to change without notice. Prices do not include sales taxes, which will be charged (if applicable) based on your state or country of residence. Canadian residents will be charged applicable taxes. Offer not valid in Quebec. This offer is limited to one order per household. Books received may not be as shown. Not valid for current subscribers to the Harlequin Special Edition or Harlequin Heartwarming series. All orders subject to approval. Credit or debit balances in a customer's account(s) may be offset by any other outstanding balance owed by or to the customer. Please allow 4 to 6 weeks for delivery. Offer available while quantities last.
Your Privacy—Your information is being collected by Harlequin Enterprises ULC, operating as Harlequin Reader Service. For a complete summary of the information we collect, how we use this information and to whom it is disclosed, please visit our privacy notice located at corporate.harlequin.com/privacy-notice. From time to time we may also exchange your personal information with reputable third parties. If you wish to opt out of this sharing of your personal information, please visit readerservice.com/consumerschoice or call 1-800-873-8635. Notice to California Residents—Under California law, you have specific rights to control and access your data. For more information on these rights and how to exercise them, visit corporate.harlequin.com/california-privacy.
HSEHW22R3